PROPAGANDA

PROPAGANDA

Jeff Gomez

For Norman Diamond

We may win this year. We may lose it all. It is not going as well as we thought.

—Renata Adler, *Speedboat*

A lot of bombs went off that Christmas in London. Every time Ron and Russell open a newspaper there are reports of a pub, government building, or shop being destroyed. News of the blasts are as common as the gray skies and light drizzle that never seem to stop. That's not even the worst of it. The Irish Civil War is raging, inflation's through the roof, and a gas shortage and walkout by the miners are slowly crippling the nation. Most people are either on strike or unemployed. In 1973, the whole country was in crisis.

The brothers had moved to Britain from Los Angeles that fall to make a fresh start. The first two Sparks LPs had tanked and, while the band managed to make some noise in the UK and Europe on their first tour last year, back in the States they were still playing to six people at the Whisky. Not good for a local band. So Ron and Russell sold most of their stuff, packed a few suitcases, and moved to London.

With a new lineup, a new label, and a new manager, things were going to be different. The only problem is they don't have any new songs. The group's slated to go into the studio in January, but all they have are a few half-written sketches and old tracks like "I Like Girls," which has been kicking around since their days at the Doggie Factory. Ron's been trying to write new material at their manager's house in Croydon, which is where they're staying, but all he has there is a guitar. Ron prefers to write on piano.

After their father died, their mom remarried and moved to London with her new husband. He's a nice guy, works in a shoe store. They've lived here a few years now, renting a modest home in Clapham Junction, three streets down from the huge tube station. The house came with a piano, so Ron travels there on Sundays, sometimes with Russell in tow, sometimes alone. When Russell tags along, he chats with their mom in the kitchen while Ron plays, hums, and scribbles in the living room. Russell tries to sneak a listen to what his brother's working on, guessing how high his voice will have to go this time. Ron's songs might be difficult to sing, but they're never boring. That's why Russell loves being in a band with him.

Sometimes, to take a break, they walk the nearby streets. Lavender Hill, Falcon Road, Parma Crescent. The brothers don't talk much on these walks—they both know what's at stake. Ron, almost thirty, feels the pressure more. If things don't work out this time, he'll have to give up music and get a job in graphic design, like his father. Russell, good-looking and only twenty-three, has more options. Filmmaking, maybe. Or fashion. Sometimes they walk as far as Battersea Park and stare into the Thames. The murky water is nothing like the churning surf they grew up with in Southern California, first in Pacific Palisades and then Venice. Even when they'd lived in Culver City, they could walk to the ocean in a half hour. They see water a lot in London—the band rehearses in a dingy room on King's Road—so they travel back and forth over the Thames almost every day. Staring into the river always makes them long for the ocean, the same way the cloudy London sky makes them miss the sunshine of California.

Besides, even if Ron manages to write enough songs for the record, there's no guarantee people will hear it. Electrical outages are affecting everything and, due to the oil shortage, vinyl records are getting thinner and thinner (when they're produced at all). Soccer matches have been moved to the afternoon, so fields won't have to be lit up at night. Electric heating has been turned off in office buildings. When Ron and Russell walk by a travel agency or bank, they see employees huddled in anoraks or just blankets. The only workplaces immune to the restrictions are those deemed essential, such as hospitals and supermarkets. In homes, power's often unavailable at night and the TV stations have a 10:30 p.m. curfew. The government's even begun to run huge ads in newspapers encouraging people to conserve power. THINK

BEFORE YOU SWITCH ON. One energy minister asked people to brush their teeth in the dark. Streetlights don't go on, giving whole neighborhoods a shadowy noir feel. Ron and Russell walk around at night with their collars turned up, like they're characters in *The Third Man*.

Big sellers that Christmas were candles and bikes. Not because people wanted to give them as gifts, but so they could light their homes or get from one place to another. Gas stations hang homemade signs on pumps reading SORRY SOLD OUT. Things are so bad the government recently announced that, starting on New Year's Day, all businesses must shift to a three-day week. Ron and Russell stared at the headlines, dumbfounded. ALL BRITAIN ON HALF TIME. THREE-DAY WEEK BY LAW! BIG SHUTDOWN IS ON THE WAY. It'd been their dream for years to be an "English band." All their heroes came from here. The Beatles, the Who, the Kinks. But lately the brothers had been wondering what in the hell they've gotten themselves into.

"So then, how are the new tracks coming, Ron?"

It's a Tuesday night and their manager is driving them to Chelsea to rehearse.

Sitting in the front seat, and barely audible above the radio playing Wizzard's "Angel Fingers," Ron says, "They're coming. Slowly but surely."

"Good. Just keep your fingers crossed the power's not cut tonight."

Russell, in the back seat, watches the streets go by. King's Road had once been the bright and shiny epicenter of the Swinging Sixties, a fashion mecca teeming with boutiques and salons. But where mods in suits once walked arm in arm with women in brightly colored miniskirts, skinheads now sullenly lean against unlit lampposts wearing Fred Perry polos, Dr. Martens, and clip-on suspenders. The streets are dirty, businesses run-down, windows shattered or boarded up.

The manager pulls up to the building. A huge sign at the top says FURNITURE CAVE OPEN 10–6. The practice space is in the basement.

"I'm going to run some errands and pick you up in a few hours. We'll grab a bite after, yeah?"

The brothers nod and get out of the car.

Russell leads the way down the stairs, a long scarf trailing after him. As they approach the door, they can hear the band running through Ron's latest creation, a fast tune in the key of A with the working title "Too Hot to Handle."

Russell holds open the door for his brother. The band is arranged in a semi-circle of bass, drums, guitar. Ron's electric piano sits opposite the door. In the center of the room is a microphone stand. The band acknowledge the brothers with nods, continuing to play.

The room is damp and cold, an electric heater in the corner doing nothing to warm the large space. The stained carpet smells of cheap lager. Wimpy wrappers spill out from an overstuffed bin. A pile of coins sits atop the electricity meter on the wall.

Martin Gordon, the bass player, is the youngest member of the group at nineteen. At his audition he had long hair like a hippie. The siblings were pleased when he showed up to his first rehearsal with short hair—not as short as Ron's, but close. As he plucks out notes on his Rickenbacker, he locks eyes with the drummer, Dinky Diamond.

Dinky, whose real name is Norman—people call him Dinky because he's small—honed his chops on the German cabaret circuit. Their manager likes to tell people he discovered Dinky in a pub in Aldershot playing Sparks tunes in a cover band. Dinky's always too good-natured to deny it.

Guitarist Adrian Fisher joined after answering an ad in *Melody Maker* that read *Sparks requires lead guitarist. Must be incredible looking and an exciting, accomplished guitarist. (Previous applicants need not apply.)* When it came time to sign contracts, he's the only one who had it looked at by a lawyer.

As Ron takes off his sweater and sits down at the piano, he notices Adrian has placed a lit cigarette behind the strings in the headstock of his black Gibson Les Paul. Ron always hates when he does that. This is Sparks, not the Stones.

When the song ends, the three band members look to the brothers, awaiting their verdict.

"Not bad," declares Ron. "But should we run through it a few more times?"

Everyone nods as Russell unwinds the scarf from his neck and grabs the microphone.

Dinky counts off with his drumsticks.

"One, two, three—"

BOOM!

A huge explosion rocks the room. Ron's knocked off his piano stool while Russell's thrown to the ground. The noise is the loudest thing the siblings have ever heard, and they saw the Beatles at the height of Beatlemania, the crowd noise like a jet engine. The two guitarists crouch, clutching their instruments while Dinky covers his ears with a drumstick in each hand, the sticks appearing to grow out of his head like antennae. An exposed light bulb hanging from the ceiling swings back and forth as dust falls from new cracks.

"What was that," Russell says in amazement, "an earthquake?"

"Goddamn Californians," spits Adrian as he puts down his electric guitar and rushes out of the practice space. Martin follows suit as Dinky jumps out from behind his drums. The three of them head upstairs to see what happened. After they're gone, Ron stares at Russell and Russell stares back. Finally, they both shrug their shoulders and trail after the band, climbing the steps to the surface two at a time.

Aboveground, the smoke is just beginning to clear. The entire front of the World's End pub two doors down has been blown apart. Shattered bricks and broken glass litter the street. The smell of cordite and burnt flesh hangs in the air. Sirens wail in the distance, slowly getting closer.

"Bloody hell," Dinky says, walking toward the rubble.

Mangled bodies writhe under bits of splintered wood and chunks of plaster. Soot-blackened hands reach out, some missing fingers, some arms just stumps. Across the street, the top of a car has been completely torn off. Adrian and Martin wade into the scene, offering help and pulling victims to safety.

As Ron and Russell warily approach the mayhem, a man emerges from the shadows. He begins to quickly walk away, crossing the street, hands shoved deep into his pockets. Ron gets a good look at him as he passes in front of an approaching fire truck. He's young and his fiery red hair is cut short. His face is a map of freckles, lips curled into a sick kind of grin. The man continues to walk, the only figure retreating from the scene as dozens of people from homes and businesses nearby rush to assist and aid the wounded.

"Ron!" Russell shouts as he begins to pull away debris. "Come help!"

Ron turns from the retreating man to what remains of the pub. The jukebox—still playing loudly in the back of the bar—can be heard over the moans of the victims. The song is Slade's recent Christmas no. 1, "Merry Xmas Everybody." Noddy Holder's voice blares out in the night: "Everybody's having fun. Look to the future now, it's only just begun."

1.
THE
CALL

"Dinky's going to be late."

Russell says this as he winds a long white scarf around his neck and walks from his bedroom to the living room. The scarf matches his white pants. Ron, sitting in an armchair in the corner, looks up from the notebook he's writing in. He's halfway through a new song about an unhappy family named Aaron, Betty, and Charlie.

"What the hell is it this time?" Ron asks.

"Didn't say," Russell answers. "He was at a phone booth by the side of the road. Could barely hear him above the traffic."

Dinky lives an hour and a half away in Hampshire. Most days he picks them up on the way into the studio, saving the brothers from having to take a bus or the tube. Because Dinky's usually late by five or ten minutes, Ron and Russell don't even bother to wait on the street at the appointed time.

They just stay in the apartment and wait for the drummer to pull up in his teal Humber Super Snipe and honk. That's when Ron and Russell finally gather their things and go downstairs.

"Phone box," Ron corrects. "Here it's known as a phone box, not a phone booth."

It's now late summer, 1974. A lot has happened since Christmas. Their debut album for Island Records, *Kimono My House*, came out in the spring and was an almost instant success. The LP's first single, "This Town Ain't Big Enough for Both of Us," rocketed to no. 2 on the charts, propelled by an appearance on *Top of the Pops* during which Russell stomped and cavorted around the stage while Ron stayed as still as a statue and pulled faces, scaring schoolkids everywhere. The brothers couldn't believe the song was a hit—it didn't sound like anything else on the radio. Then again, maybe that's why it was a hit. "Amateur Hour" was quickly released as a follow-up and was also a hit, even without *Top of the Pops* (the show was off the air for almost two months due to a strike by BBC technicians). Cashing in on their success, an old record label reissued a track from their second album, "Girl from Germany," and even that was selling. The brothers were everywhere. Magazine covers, TV shows, radio interviews. Fans began to follow them around. The subsequent tour in June and July was also a massive success. Tickets to a concert in Hull sold out in an hour and a half, and the final night at the Rainbow sold out in a week. Girls screamed and invaded the stage, pawing at Russell and even Ron. They'd seen it happen to other bands, including their beloved Beatles. Now it was happening to them. Not bad for a group nobody had heard of just a few months ago.

"So, what should we do?" Russell sits down in an overstuffed chair and picks at a piece of lint on his tomato-soup-red sweater. "Dinky said he won't be here for at least another hour."

Since moving out of their manager's house, the brothers have been renting a two-bedroom flat in Beckenham. They like it. There are plenty of good Indian restaurants in the neighborhood, a few bookstores, a record store, and a movie theater that shows old films. The band's just starting to record their second album for Island at AIR Studios in central London, right off Oxford Circus.

"I'm hungry," Ron says, closing the notebook.

"Want to go to the hotel?" Russell suggests. Three doors down, there's a large hotel with a restaurant just off the lobby. The brothers often go there for breakfast on the weekends.

Grabbing a pair of black designer sunglasses, Ron says, "Sure." He's wearing a blue sweater, white shirt, black tie, and blue slacks.

Russell rips a piece of paper from a small notepad, jots down the number to the studio from their address book, and puts the slip of paper in his pocket.

They exit the flat and walk toward the hotel. On a

boarded-up window in between the apartment building and the hotel someone has spray-painted ENOCH WAS RIGHT. The morning, even though it's still summer, is cool and brisk. Clouds in the sky look like they might give way to sun later.

The brothers enter the hotel lobby. The restaurant is just beyond a small sitting room with a bank of phones and a wire rack holding brochures for tourist attractions. They enter the restaurant and take their usual table that looks out onto the street. A waiter approaches and takes their order. Tea, toast, and a plate of fruit.

It's almost ten on a Thursday, so the restaurant is mostly empty. The few people in the room have finished their meals and are now reading the paper, faces obscured by newsprint. Russell squints and reads a headline: ONE DEAD IN TOWER CARNAGE. MAIMING OF THE INNOCENTS.

"The Tower of London was bombed yesterday."

"I know," Ron says. "I heard it on the news last night. One dead. Forty-one injured."

Russell shakes his head. The bombings, which have been a feature of their time in Britain, haven't let up. But it's not just pubs anymore. Last month the Houses of Parliament was hit and, before that, four people were injured when a bomb went off at Heathrow.

Mention of the attack makes Ron think of last December, the pub in Chelsea. He can't get out of his mind the face of the red-haired man he saw leaving the wreckage. No one had died that night, but dozens were hurt. The brothers and the rest of the band had stayed for hours to help the victims and to clean up. It had shocked Ron and Russell to witness such violence. The images haunted them for days. Back in the States the brothers had participated in demonstrations against the war in Vietnam and once—in Century City protesting a fundraiser for Lyndon Johnson—they'd been chased by police waving billy clubs. But that was nothing like this. If he tries, Ron can still remember the smell of burning flesh.

The food arrives and Russell eagerly digs in. Ron reaches only for the tea.

"Excuse me, you're Sparks, aren't you?"

They look up to see a young man in a long coat carrying a copy of the *NME*. He's thin and pale with longish brown hair. He looks to be about fourteen or fifteen.

"Yes, that's us," Ron says, putting down his tea.

Being recognized had taken some getting used to. It was strange at first, and overwhelming when it was dozens of screaming girls, especially since—once they'd cornered the brothers—they didn't know quite what to do with them. Ron wears dark sunglasses in order to achieve some semblance of anonymity, but the toothbrush mustache always gives him away.

"I-I wrote this about you."

Russell reads it while the young man looks away,

embarrassed. *Today I bought the album of the year. I feel I can say this without expecting several letters saying I'm talking rubbish. The album is* Kimono My House *by Sparks. I bought it on the strength of the single, but every track is brilliant.* Finished, Russell hands it to his brother.

While Ron's looking it over, Russell asks the young man, "What's your name?"

"Steven," he says shyly. "I came down from Manchester on the train, and I-I just want to say that you have the most beautiful female voice in pop music."

Russell is about to say thank you when, at the table behind them, a woman fumbles with a cut-glass ashtray, dropping it to the tiled floor. When both brothers look her way, the young man snatches back the *NME*, along with a crust of Russell's toast, and slinks out of the dining room.

Russell jumps out of his chair and joins the woman under the table to help pick up the big chunks of broken glass.

"Oh, thank you," she says. Their hands briefly touch as they reach for the same shard near one of the table legs. "I don't know what happened. I was just trying to move it when it slipped and fell."

They stand and put the broken pieces on the table. Two waiters, one armed with a small broom and dustpan, clean up the ashes and take the bits of glass away. When the girl sits back down, Russell joins her. So does Ron, to the annoyance of Russell.

"Quite a commotion," Ron says.

The woman's wearing a short, floral-printed dress. Her black hair is cut in a page boy style. Russell's curly hair is longer.

"You're Americans," she says, a smile appearing on her face.

"Yes," Russell says, adding, "we're from California."

"That's just brilliant," she replies, her voice rising an octave or two. "I've always wanted to go there. Tell me, is it just like a Beach Boys song? With everybody tanned and surfing all of the time?"

"Not everybody surfs," Ron answers. "In fact, the Beach Boys don't even surf, apart from the drummer."

She laughs, covering her mouth with her hand when she does so. The brothers like her laugh.

Russell notices the two plates containing remnants of an English breakfast.

"It looks like you've already eaten," he says, "but would you like to join us for a cup of tea?"

"I'd love to, but can't. I was only meant to have a quick catch-up with an old friend while I was in the area running an errand, but we just kept on talking and talking. I'm well late as it is."

"Shame," Ron says. "Maybe some other time?"

She smiles and begins to search for something in her purse. She pulls out a pen.

"I'll give you my number. Do you have something I can write on?"

Russell quickly digs into his pocket and pulls out the piece of paper. He finds the blank side and hands it to her. She quickly scribbles something and hands it back.

"Here's my number at the office. Call me sometime."

"Where do you work?" says Ron.

"Department of Trade."

Looking at the slip of paper, Russell says, "Wow, that must be interesting."

"Not for me, I'm just a secretary. My boss gets to go to meetings in fun and exotic places. I just make the arrangements." She points to a bulging envelope under her purse. "I just picked these up. Plane tickets. Trade conference in Spain."

"Don't you ever get to go on those trips?" Ron says.

"No, but I won't be a secretary forever." She glances at a tiny wristwatch. "Oh, wow, I really do need to go."

She flashes them both a smile before throwing down a few coins and running from the room. The brothers rise and watch her walk out of the restaurant. Russell hands the piece of paper to Ron. Her handwriting is all circles. It's almost hard to read her name written above the numbers.

"Siobhán," Ron says.

They return to their own table. The waiter comes by and refreshes their tea.

"Siobhán," Russell repeats, taking back the slip of paper.

A half hour later, after the waiter's cleared away the dishes and the brothers can't drink any more tea, Russell turns to Ron.

"Still no Dinky."

Ron looks out the window and watches cars go by in both directions, every third or fourth one a boxy black cab. There's no sign of the teal Humber. As he's staring, a maroon Rover pulls up and obscures his view. Three huge guys get out. When one of them sneezes, it's so loud and violent Ron can hear it through the glass. Turning back to his brother, he sees that Russell's holding the slip of paper with the phone numbers on it.

"Should we call the studio?" Ron says. "Muff's probably getting worried about us."

Muff—whose real name is Mervyn—is the older brother of Steve Winwood. They both got their start in the Spencer Davis Group in the sixties, Muff playing bass and Steve on keyboards. By the end of the decade, Muff had transitioned to the business side of the industry, working behind the scenes as a producer and A&R man. His younger brother went on to achieve chart success with his new band, Traffic. Ron sometimes looks at the producer, wondering if he'll share the same fate. There could be worse things.

"Sure, let me go call him," Russell says.

As his brother's standing up, Ron says, "Just the studio, okay? Don't call that girl."

Russell puts the bit of paper in his pocket and flashes his

best smile.

"Would I do a thing like that? Without telling you?"

"Yes, you would."

Russell continues to smile as he exits the dining room. Entering the small space off the lobby with the phones, a huge guy wearing a dark suit pulls Russell aside and shoves something hard into his stomach. The man's name is Rocco.

"What the—"

Russell turns. He's startled by the huge scar running down the left side of Rocco's pudgy face.

"Shut it, mate. I've got a gun against your ribs, so keep your mouth shut and come with me."

As he nervously looks around for help, Russell sees Ron being pushed through the lobby, two scary-looking guys on either side of him. Both are wearing dark suits. The one with a black tie is Archie. The one with a red tie is Tommy.

"Where are they taking my brother?"

"Don't you worry about that none." Rocco's thick Cockney accent makes *you* sound like *ooo*. "We 'ave space enough for you both."

"But we have—the studio . . ."

As he begins to struggle, still not sure what's going on, Rocco places his other hand on Russell's upper arm and begins shoving him through the lobby. Russell looks around desperately, hoping someone behind the front desk, or maybe a waiter or bellboy, will see what's happening and intervene. But the lobby's deserted.

Out on the sidewalk, the passenger door is open on the maroon Rover. Archie and Tommy are in the front. Russell can see, through the rear window, Ron's blue sweater and the back of his head. Honking comes from down the street but, as Russell turns to see where it's coming from, Rocco grabs him by the shoulders.

"Mind your pretty head, duchess," he grumbles as he shoves Russell into the Rover and slides in beside him. The car speeds away from the curb, merging into traffic, before the door is even closed.

The M16's been screwing up Dinky since they started recording the album. Construction started last year on the new ring road that will encircle all of London, and every day it seems there's some obstacle stopping him from picking up the brothers on time. Three lanes going down to one, huge trucks piled with gear slowing down traffic, or just being stopped altogether for no apparent reason. The road will be great once it's finished, but for now it's one big pain in his ass.

Today, Dinky's view out the windshield is a sea of blinking brake lights. Cars inch forward every few seconds before having to stop again. It's taken almost ten minutes to go just half a kilometer. The drummer in him tries to count time—looking for the rhythm in the starting and stopping—but it's too staccato, too random. Too much like jazz. He likes rock and roll. Instead, he thinks about the new record.

The first couple of weeks in the studio have been great, a total reversal from when they recorded the last one. *Kimono* had been done under a cloud of unease and doubt. Ron and Russell were still getting used to London, the three-day week wreaked havoc with the schedule, and Muff was feeling out everyone's individual style. And while the songs sounded good to them, no one was quite sure they'd sound good to anyone else. After all, you don't normally hear songs about Albert Einstein on the radio. But the record came out and was a big hit.

Of course, there have been changes since then. Bass player Martin Gordon is no longer in the group. Ron and Russell never did like the sound of his Rickenbacker, and Martin resisted moving to a Fender. A replacement was found close to home. Their manager, John Hewlett—who'd been in the band John's Children the previous decade—had created a group called Jook around singer-songwriter Ian Kimmet. To complete the lineup, Hewlett added Ian Hampton on bass and Trevor White on guitar, as well as John's Children's former drummer, Chris Townson. Jook gigged and recorded a couple of singles, but never saw much success. Earlier this summer, once everyone involved could tell that the band wasn't going to make it, Hewlett persuaded Hampton— along with White—to leave Jook and join Sparks. Jook disbanded shortly after.

Ian and Trevor fit in right away. They're both a year older than Ron, so they're mature and professional. They show up on time and get the job done. Arranging the new songs has been easy; Adrian's handling the leads and Trevor's playing rhythm. Meanwhile, Dinky and Ian have formed a close bond, the way a rhythm section should. And even though it's been barely two weeks since the tour ended, they've been in the studio nearly every day since. Ron just keeps coming up with songs; Dinky's not quite sure how.

The logjam finally breaks, the cars begin to move, and Dinky concentrates again on the road. In no time he turns off the highway and onto the streets of Beckenham.

Finally turning onto Ron and Russell's street, he glances at his wristwatch: 11:16 a.m. He's even later than he told Russell he'd be.

"The boys are going to kill me."

He pulls up alongside their building and gives a quick honk. When they don't come down, he honks again. Nothing.

Dinky rolls down his window and looks up to the third story. Sometimes, when he arrives late, he'll look up and see one or both brothers standing there, shaking their heads. Today, after a few beats and when no one comes to either the window or out of the building, he says, "I bet they got tired of waiting and took a cab."

Dinky puts the car in gear and is about to leave when,

down the block, he sees Ron leave the hotel flanked by Archie and Tommy. Ron doesn't look happy, not that he ever looks that happy. Tommy opens the rear passenger door to the Rover, while Archie gets behind the wheel. After Ron's shoved inside, Tommy runs around the back of the car and sits next to Archie. A few seconds later, Russell exits the hotel standing closer than necessary to Rocco. Even from half a block away Dinky can see the large scar traveling all the way down Rocco's face.

"Who are those geezers?"

Rocco pushes Russell into the back seat and then gets in himself, the Rover taking off with one of the back doors still open. The car merges clumsily with traffic, having to swerve to avoid a driver coming in the opposite direction and cutting off a truck turning from a side street.

Dinky sits there for a few seconds, his engine noisily idling, wondering what to do.

"Guess I'd better see where they're going," he finally says. "Muff will give me an earful if I show up without the songwriters."

Checking his side-view mirror, Dinky pulls into traffic and follows the Rover.

◍

They've been driving for nearly ten minutes, but no one's said anything. The smell of cheap aftershave mixed with stale cigarette smoke fills the interior of the car. The two goons in the front stare out the window impassively, while Rocco only grunts in response to Russell elbowing him to get more room in the cramped space. Ron finally breaks the silence.

"I didn't pay."

Rocco leans forward.

"What'd you just say?"

"Back there." Ron cocks his head toward the hotel that's now miles away. "We were just finishing breakfast, but you kidnapped us before I had a chance to pay."

Rocco just glares, his scar appearing to almost glow.

"My brother's right," adds Russell. "And we like that place. We don't want to create any problems."

"Listen, mate," Tommy says from the front seat in an accent even thicker than Rocco's, "you're going to be the one with the problem if you don't cooperate with us, understand?"

"Okay," Ron says, "but if we can't go to that hotel anymore because of this, it's going to be your fault."

Stopped behind a red light, all three thugs laugh. The light turns green, the Rover speeds up, and there's silence in the car again.

As they're driven through London, Ron and Russell turn their heads and peer out the window. Neither are exactly sure where they are. All London neighborhoods look relatively the same: terraced houses, chip shops, greengrocers, pubs.

The brothers have gotten to know the city reasonably well during the time they've spent here, but they still have trouble telling one neighborhood or borough apart from the other. They can't tell where Mayfair ends and Soho begins, or how far into Soho you go before it turns into Marylebone. And while Ron and Russell know and recognize certain landmarks—the Bank of England, Admiralty Arch, Nelson's Column—they're not sure exactly where those landmarks are in relation to anything else. As confusing as this is, they like this about London; it reminds them of the sprawl of Los Angeles.

When the Rover crosses the Thames, the brothers realize they're being taken north. The studio can't be too far away. Ron glances at his watch. It's not quite noon. If he could persuade these guys to drop them off, explaining this is all just one big misunderstanding, he and Russell could be there by lunch.

"Excuse me," Ron says.

Rocco slowly turns his head.

"What is it now?"

"Look, I don't know who you fellas think we are, but we don't know anything."

Rocco chuckles and replies, "Oh, I figured that already."

"No, I mean—if you think we're spies or politicians or something, we're not. We're a rock group."

Rocco sits up a bit to look Ron over.

"You look like a maths teacher, mate."

Ron points to Russell. "Well, he's the singer. I just—"

"Keep a lid on it; we're almost there. All will be revealed, okay?"

Rocco's about to say something else when he unleashes a loud and terrifying sneeze.

ACHOO.

"That's a hell of a sneeze you have there," Ron says.

"Innit?"

"Summer colds are the worst," adds Russell.

"It might be the death of me," Rocco says.

Ron responds, "As long as it's not the death of us."

This time the three thugs don't laugh. Looking at the nails on his right hand—his knuckles are huge and gnarled, like a cauliflower—Rocco coolly replies, "We'll see about that."

Twenty minutes later, the Rover pulls up to a semi-detached house on a quiet side street lined with trees. The suburban nature of the destination fills both Ron and Russell with hope. Nothing bad could happen on a nice street like this.

The Rover parks behind a dark blue van. Archie kills the engine. Tommy says, "Okay, you lot, end of the line. Everybody out."

Rocco's the first one out of the car. He walks quickly past a pair of large hedges to the front door and gives three short knocks. The brothers slide out from the back seat as Archie and Tommy slowly open their doors and step onto the gravel. The burst of fresh air is welcome after the stink of the car.

Russell looks at the two goons as they lean against the Rover and light up cigarettes. They look pretty out of shape; both are at least ten or twenty pounds overweight. Their dark suits barely hide bulges. Russell was the starting quarterback in high school. He figures if he makes a run for it, he could be at the corner before the thugs even realize he's gone. They passed a shopping district a few streets back. There were restaurants and cafés and people; there might even be a policeman. Russell's trying to get Ron to look his way, so he can convey his plan, when a gun appears in his ribs.

"Now don't you try nothing clever, sweetheart."

The door's finally answered by a man wearing weathered work clothes and a black ski mask. Rocco doesn't seem to think this is weird. Ron and Russell think this is weird. After a few hushed words passed between the two men, Rocco gives a signal. Tommy and Archie quickly flick their cigarettes into the street and grab Ron and Russell, pushing them toward the house. The brothers both hesitate, walking in small, slow steps, trying to forestall the inevitable. The man with the mask steps aside to allow just the brothers to enter the house. After the door closes, they hear Rocco on the front step sneeze again.

ACHOO.

Ron and Russell look around. It appears to be a normal

London suburban home. They see a lushly appointed living room, formal dining room, part of a kitchen. Formica counters, patterned wallpaper, high-end appliances.

Another man with a mask, taller than the first, appears from somewhere inside the house. The tall one is Shane. The short one is Liam. Shane says, "Take them upstairs. Quinn will be up in a bit. But make it so they can't escape, know what I mean?"

Ron tries to place the man's accent. It's not English. It's Scottish, or maybe Irish.

Liam gives a quick nod and then pushes the brothers to a staircase covered in thick carpet. As they're walking toward the second story, Ron says, "Nice house, yours?"

Liam doesn't respond.

On the landing at the top of the stairs are three brown duffel bags. One of them is open and, when Russell looks over, he can see gleaming black metal. Weapons.

The brothers are pushed into a spacious master bedroom. In the middle of the room is an unmade king-size bed, covers pulled down revealing white sheets and pillows. To the right of the bed is an end table holding a black rotary phone. Along one wall are two wooden dressers, and along the other wall there's a steel writing desk and chair. An open door peeks into a bathroom with pink tile. The carpet here is even thicker than it was downstairs.

Liam says, "Now, get on the bed."

"Look, I don't know what you have in mind," Russell

says, "but we're brothers."

Liam moves forward menacingly.

"I don't care who ya are, I'm telling you to lay down."

"It's 'lie' down," Ron corrects.

"You want a smack?"

"No thanks."

As the brothers reluctantly crawl onto the bed and lie down, Russell asks, "Shouldn't we take our shoes off?"

But Liam's not listening. He's rifling through a dresser near the door, his back to the brothers. When he turns around, he's holding various lengths of rope.

"Now, turn over and get back-to-back."

Ron and Russell warily do what he says.

Liam proceeds to tie them up, first binding their feet before moving on to their hands. As he's wrapping the ropes around Russell's wrists, the long white scarf gets in the way. He moves on to Ron and then ties the brothers together with the last bits of rope, joining their bound hands in a series of tight knots.

"Now you stay put," Liam says, "and don't try anything funny. The boss will deal with you shortly."

He exits the room and closes the door behind him. Ron and Russell, not sure what to do, just lie there. Like in the car before, no one says anything.

In a way, they've been like this most of their lives. Tied to each other. Ever since their dad died unexpectedly when they were young—Ron was eleven, Russell only eight—

they've been a pair, a duo. They went everywhere together, did everything as a team. There was no Russell without Ron, no Ron without Russell. This continued even as adults. Russell went to UCLA because that's where his brother went. People around campus soon got used to seeing them as a unit. Those tentative first bands at college formed the template each of their groups would later follow: musicians orbiting around the inseparable nucleus of Ron and Russell. People could sense this. Ron and Russell were on their own wavelength, had their own world, and no one else could crack it. It went beyond just being brothers. The first incarnation of Sparks included another set of brothers— Earle and James Mankey—but they weren't like Ron and Russell. The Mankeys just happened to be related. The Maels make up one person.

"Can you move at all?" Ron finally says.

Russell moves his shoulders back and forth, then his arms and then his hips.

"Not much. I just did my entire Mick Jagger routine, and nothing gave."

"These guys must be sailors." Ron cranes his head, trying to get a look at their hands. "Look at these knots."

"What do you think's going on? What do these guys want?"

Ron considers this. "Maybe they're from the hotel."

Russell sighs and adds, "I really wish we would have paid."

They both wriggle and struggle some more before giving up.

"Should we try something else?" Russell says, out of breath from the effort.

"Like what?"

"I don't know, yell?"

"I suppose it wouldn't hurt," Ron says. "Although I didn't see too many cars on the street aside from the van and the one we came in. Also, it's the middle of the day."

Russell shifts and notices a large window in the corner. He says, "But there's got to be, like, housewives or something, right? One of them could call the police."

Ron considers this.

"I don't know," he says. "I'd hate to make these guys angry."

"I think they're already angry."

"Well, then," Ron says, "angrier."

"I'm going to do it," Russell finally announces. He takes a few quick breaths and then unleashes his loudest, highest wail. It's not quite a high C, but it's close.

Within seconds there are footsteps on the stairs. The door opens in a burst. It's the tall one, Shane. His eyes behind the black ski mask are narrow slits of anger.

"Pipe down, ya feckin' eejit! You want to let the whole street know you're here?"

"That was the point," Ron says. "Did it work?"

Shane goes to the window and looks out surreptitiously.

There's nothing. No front doors opening to see what the commotion was. No approaching sirens. He lets out a long sigh, goes to the dresser, and pulls out two large white handkerchiefs.

"I shoulda done this before," he says. "I was a fool to think you'd cooperate."

Shane crawls on the bed and uses the handkerchiefs to gag the brothers, Russell first and then Ron. He ties them tight, the brothers choking at first on the cotton before breathing through their noses. Shane hops off the bed and leaves the room, cursing under his breath.

After he leaves, Ron grunts something and Russell grunts something back. Ron grunts again, but soon tires of the conversation and just remains quiet.

Ten minutes later, there's a short knock before the bedroom door is opened. A man of about forty enters. This is Quinn. He has messy brown hair and a droopy mustache, and he's wearing a crumpled gray suit. Liam and Shane, still in their masks, stand on either side of the open door as Quinn pulls the chair from the desk and sits down.

"Sorry to have kept you gentlemen waiting."

Ron tries to say something, but it just comes out as muffled gibberish.

"Ah, yes," Quinn says, turning to Liam. "Will you please take off their gags?"

He steps forward, lowering first Russell's gag and then Ron's.

"Look, I don't know who you think we are," Russell says quickly, in case the gag will be returned before he has a chance to plead his case, "but you got the wrong guys. We're in a band. We're only here in London to record an album."

Quinn laughs and says, "We don't care who you are."

"What?" gasps Ron. "Then why did you kidnap us?"

"It's simple, really. We just need you to make a phone call for us."

Ron and Russell try to look at each other. It's difficult, seeing as they're tied up facing in opposite directions.

Turning back to Quinn, Ron says, "What kind of phone call?"

"Let me explain," he says. "Me and my associates here are part of what you might call a *political* organization, and tonight we're going to bomb a pub. However, in order to keep the number of casualties down—we're not animals after all—we like to call a newspaper and give them the time and the location. That way they can prepare. Clear the place out."

"But if you're going to warn people, and announce that the pub's going to be bombed," Russell says, "why bomb it at all? What's that going to accomplish?"

"It sends a message."

"But someone could still get killed," Russell says.

"Well, then," Quinn replies without emotion, "that becomes part of the message."

As he gets up and retrieves the telephone from the end table, Ron asks, "Why don't you just make the call yourself?"

"We don't want to be identified." Quinn places the phone on the bed next to Ron's head. "You see, this isn't exactly the first time we've done this. The authorities are keen to know who we are, and we'd rather keep that a secret. So, we thought this time we'd, well, get a volunteer to do it for us. That's why you're here."

"But why do you need both of us?" says Russell, struggling once again with the ropes. His arms are beginning to cramp from being in the same position for so long.

"We don't, really. Bit of a mix-up on the part of our associates. I apologize."

"You mean the guys downstairs?" Ron says, pointing with his bound feet. "They work for you?"

"Not exactly," Quinn says, sitting back down on the chair. "Our organization has a bit of overlap with theirs, so we're forced to work together from time to time. Strange bedfellows and all that."

"Why would they believe us?" Russell says.

"What's that?"

"The call, the phone call you want us to make. Why won't the newspaper or whatever just think it's a hoax. Teenagers or something. A prank."

"Well, like I said, this isn't the first time we've done this. And we've come to, I guess you could call it, an *arrangement* with the authorities. There's a code word that we know and that they know, and as long as that code word is used, they'll know the call's from us and that it's legitimate."

"Even if we're the ones who make the call," Russell says warily.

"Exactly." Quinn pulls a piece of paper folded in thirds from his blazer. "I have it all written down right here. Won't take but a second."

"And if we make the call," Ron says hopefully, "you'll let us go?"

"Well, let me put it this way: if you *don't* make the call, there's no chance you're going to leave this house alive."

The brothers' minds begin to race. Russell still can't tell whether any of this is real. The past six months—the success of the band, the single hitting no. 2, the sold-out tour— have made life seem like a dream; maybe this is part of that dream. Meanwhile, Ron's trying to dig into who these guys really are. Quinn's accent seems to slip. Sometimes he sounds Irish and sometimes he doesn't.

"Are you the IRA?" Ron says.

Quinn, unfolding the piece of paper, replies, "Does it matter?"

Without waiting for an answer, he rises from the chair and places the paper next to Ron. When he picks up the telephone receiver, Ron hears that strange English dial tone.

"So, what do you say, lads? Will you do us this favor?"

Ron looks from the letter to Quinn and then back to the letter.

"I don't believe you."

"Don't believe what, son?"

"The bomb, the letter, any of it."

Russell wriggles in the ropes, trying to send his brother a message. Whether or not the bomb exists, the gun that had been stuck into his ribs a short while ago was real.

Quinn sighs and places the receiver back onto the phone.

"Liam, will you please show this gentleman we mean business?"

The masked man retreats into the hallway. He returns a few seconds later with two of the brown duffel bags they'd seen before on the landing. He unzips one slowly before moving on to the next. He picks up each bag and shows it to Ron and then Russell. They see wires, alarm clocks, and a whole lot of duct tape. Bombs.

Ron thinks back to Christmas, the pub that was blown apart on King's Road. The screams, the smell of burnt flesh. The lives that were shattered. And for what?

As Liam is zipping up the bags, Ron says slowly, "No."

"What's that, lad? I couldn't quite hear you."

Liam retreats into the hallway with the duffel bags and doesn't return.

"I said no," Ron repeats. "We won't be a party to your propaganda."

Quinn reaches into his blazer again. This time he pulls out a gun. He rises from the chair and approaches the bed. He places the short nose of the black revolver against Russell's forehead. Russell sniffs and can smell oil on the gun.

"Then let me put it this way, mate. If you *don't* make the

call, I'll redecorate the walls with your friend's brain. Do I make myself clear?"

Quinn cocks the gun. The loud click sounds just like it does in the movies.

"Okay, I'll do it," Ron says, his voice cracking. "Just don't hurt my brother."

Quinn returns the gun to his blazer.

"I knew you'd listen to reason." He reaches for the phone, but then stops. "Actually, you have a shite voice. Let's have the pretty one here make the call."

Quinn reaches for the phone and places it near Russell's head. "Dial it for me, will you, Shane?"

As Shane comes forward, Quinn momentarily puts down the piece of paper so he can stuff the handkerchief back into Ron's mouth. Ron tries to struggle against this, wiggling and writhing impotently, but it does no good. The gag is soon in place again. Shane dials the number while Quinn retrieves the paper and holds it where Russell can see. The phone is laid to rest on the bed beside Russell's head. Ron, gagged and still in his sunglasses, strapped to his brother, lies mutely.

"Just read it the way it is here. They'll know what to do on the other side, okay?"

"Don't I get a chance to rehearse?" Russell asks. "Do a couple of warm-ups? A run-through?"

Exasperated, Quinn says, "It's a bomb threat, ducky, not a school play. Just read."

Russell's looking over the text when the ringing stops and a voice answers.

"*Evening Standard* city desk, how can I help you?"

The voice, a woman's, is bright and chipper. She sounds young.

Russell, his eyes fixed on the paper, freezes.

"Hello? Is anyone there?"

Quinn reaches into his suit with his free hand. The gun is halfway out when Russell finally speaks.

"Yes, uh, hello . . . this—this is a warning. A bomb will be placed today at the Tattersalls Tavern. It is due to go off at eighteen hundred hours."

"Yes, the Tattersalls Tavern. A bomb." The brightness from a few moments ago is gone. The woman now sounds scared. "Eighteen hundred hours."

"Good," Russell says. "And, uh—I have one more thing to say. Hippopotamus."

"Hippopotamus, got it."

Shane hangs up and places the phone back onto the end table. As Quinn folds up the paper and places it into his pocket, Liam enters the room.

"Is it done?"

"It's done," says Quinn. All three of them begin to laugh.

Russell asks, confused, "What's so funny?"

Wiping tears from his eyes, Quinn replies, "Well, thanks to you, half of the London police force will be in Knightsbridge tonight at that silly pub while we're across town focusing on the real target."

"Real target?" Russell asks, his voice straining. "And what's that?"

"The Prince of Wales. You see, it *was* a hoax, and you just helped us."

Russell starts to say something when Shane lunges forward and replaces his gag.

Quinn is leaving the room when Liam stops him and motions to Ron and Russell.

"What do we do with the Yanks? Clive said no loose ends."

"You're right. We better kill them."

Hearing this, Ron and Russell begin to frantically squirm on the bed, not that it does any good.

"But they're in a band," Liam protests. "Won't someone miss them?"

"You believed that nonsense? Band, my arse," Quinn sniffs. "They're just a couple of ponces mincing about talking rubbish."

"Band or not, they're Americans. We can't just dump them in Leicester Square like they're a couple of tearaways from the East End."

Quinn contemplates this for a minute.

"Have our associates downstairs deliver them to Des. He'll know how to handle a delicate situation like this."

As Quinn leaves the room, the two masked men reach for the brothers. They manage to get them on their feet and, with considerable difficulty, march them slowly down the stairs. Just outside the front door, Russell's scarf gets caught on a hedge.

"You and your bloody scarf," Shane barks, pulling it away.

The three thugs, who had all been leaning against the Rover smoking cigarettes, snap to attention. Stepping forward, Rocco asks, "Where to now, chief?"

"Drop them off at Des's. He'll know what to do." Liam removes a hand from Ron's shoulder so he can dig into his pocket. He pulls out a pair of car keys and tosses them to Archie. "Take the van."

Rocco frowns and asks, "Why can't we just take our car?"

"Too indiscreet," Liam says, nodding toward the Rover. "I don't want anyone to see 'em. The van's better. Just bring it right back after, yeah?"

Archie runs to get behind the wheel as Liam and Shane carry the brothers to the back of the van. Rocco opens the double doors and helps the two masked men wrangle the brothers. Ron and Russell continue twisting and shimmying, trying to escape, only it's no use. They're tossed into the back of the van like a couple of sofas.

Dinky's wishing he had something to eat. It's now almost one o'clock and he's been in his car outside the house in the suburbs for over an hour. If it had been a normal day, and they were in the studio, the teaboy would have been sent out for sandwiches or a curry or something. Instead, Dinky's just sitting there, getting hungrier and hungrier. He would leave to grab a bite somewhere; a few streets back, before they turned into this neighborhood, he passed a kebab shop. But he doesn't want to leave until he finds out what's happening to Ron and Russell.

Ever since marching the brothers into the house, the three goons from the hotel have done nothing but stand around and lean against the maroon Rover. Once or twice, they did a little something to break the monotony. Archie and Tommy sparred for a bit, Rocco went into the house only to return a minute later, and all three have each smoked half a dozen cigarettes. Otherwise, nothing much has happened.

Dinky looks in the glove compartment, seeing if he has a bag of crisps or a packet of biscuits or something. There's nothing but a few maps, some drumsticks, an oily rag, and two pairs of sunglasses. Digging deeper he feels something cold. Steel. He pulls it out.

"Blimey," he says.

In his hand is a small, two-barreled Derringer pistol. It's gold with mother-of-pearl inlay on the handle. Dinky forgot he had it. An old bandmate had given it to him years ago, when he was spending a lot of time playing seedy clubs out in the middle of nowhere. "You're not ever going to have to use it," his friend had said. "Just wave it about. That'll be enough to get you out of trouble." Dinky accepted the handgun at the time, but quickly stowed it away in his car, where he promptly forgot about it. He now puts it back, placing it under the folded maps and sunglasses. He closes the glove box and turns again to the three thugs.

"These blokes look like gangsters to me," he says under his breath. "But what could they want with Ron and Russell?"

This doesn't make any sense to Dinky. The brothers don't even drink or smoke, let alone do something like gamble. When they'd been led from the car to the house, Dinky could have sworn he saw one of the goons carrying a gun. On tour, the brothers never even joined the water-pistol fights on the bus. And when the band's out at a pub, having a pint to unwind after a show, the brothers are already back at the hotel, reading. They're the last two people on Earth who'd be mixed up with guys like these.

Dinky looks up and down the street. Other than the occasional car going by in either direction, there's no noise or movement anywhere. A bird squawked a while ago, but only once. And other than the van and the Rover, there are no cars parked on the street. The neighborhood feels like a ghost town.

Dinky focuses on the van. It's a battered old Commer, the kind that English bands everywhere use for touring. He's spent countless hours in the back of vans like that, heading up and down the country on the way to gigs. Sometimes groups make shelves in the back, storing instruments below and sleeping on top. Dinky often saw the sun rise through the windshield of a Commer while clinging to a beer-soaked blanket. Not anymore. For the Sparks tour, they'd hired a forty-one-seat coach. Dinky felt like he'd finally made it.

At the house, there's some movement. Dinky can see the front door open over the top of the tall hedges. Someone's coming out. The three gangsters suddenly look alive, extinguishing their cigarettes. Dinky strains but can see only the tops of heads, all of them moving slowly.

When the figures appear at the street, Dinky first notices the two men wearing black balaclavas in addition to flared jeans and work shirts.

"Jesus, now what?" Dinky sighs.

Then he spots Ron and Russell. It takes him a second to recognize them since the brothers are bound and gagged and are being helped along by the two guys in masks.

Some words are exchanged, but Dinky's too far away to hear what's being said. Rocco opens the back of the van and helps the masked men load the brothers in. As Rocco closes the doors, Dinky hears him sneeze.

ACHOO.

The gangsters get in the van as Liam and Shane return to the house. The van starts up and pulls away from the curb, leaving behind the maroon Rover. When the van turns around and passes the Humber, Dinky sits down low in his seat so the driver doesn't see him. When the van's at the end of the street, Dinky sits up quickly and starts his car. The engine knocks as it roars to life. In his side-view mirror, he sees the van take a right turn. He puts the Humber in gear and follows.

The smell is back, only this time the stale scent of cigarette smoke is overpowering the goons' fading aftershave. Rocco is in the rear with Ron and Russell, while Tommy and Archie are in the front seats. The radio's on and Tommy hums along to "Open Up" by Mungo Jerry.

After just a few turns, Rocco stands up, balancing himself against the swaying of the van. Leaning over, he pushes down the gags on Ron and then Russell.

"Those blokes back there may not have been able to handle you," he says as he sits back down. "But we can. We've seen much worse than you lot, believe me."

The brothers' jaws are sore, their throats dry. They both open and close their mouths, trying to get feeling back into the lower parts of their faces.

Once he can move his tongue again, Ron says, "Thank you."

"Yes, thank you," adds Russell.

"Think nothing of it." Rocco leans back against the wall of the van. "Might as well settle in, boys. It's a long ride."

The brothers do their best to get comfortable. After a few minutes of writhing and scooting, they manage to push themselves up against the side of the van, their legs splayed out in opposite directions. Ron, turning his head, can see mostly blue sky from the van's back windows along with streetlights and the corners of buildings passing by.

ACHOO.

The sneeze is so violent Rocco's pitched forward, hair falling into his face. He wipes his nose on his sleeve, leaving a trail of mucous on his dark suit. With his other hand he pushes back his hair.

"I think we just passed a Boots," Ron says. "Feel free to stop and get something for your cold."

Rocco ignores this and pulls a pack of Everest cigarettes from his hip pocket and lights one. This prompts Tommy and Archie in the front seats to do the same. In no time, the van is filled with smoke.

"So, you're Americans," Rocco says. "Where you from, exactly?"

"Los Angeles," Russell says.

Rocco's face lights up.

"Hollywood! I knew it—that's why you're wearing the sunglasses. Know any movie stars?"

"Well, actually," Ron begins, "Doris Day is our mother."

Rocco laughs, takes a drag from his cigarette, and then calls out to the front, "Fellas, these two daft cunts just told me their mum's Doris Day! Do you think we oughta forget Des and try and get a few bob for 'em on the open market?"

Archie doesn't respond and Tommy just shrugs.

"Guess we'll just stick to the plan, then."

After a few more turns, Archie calls out, "Boss, we're being followed."

Rocco gets up and, again balancing himself against the movement of the van, walks carefully to the back doors. He peers out sideways, so he won't be seen.

"Do you blokes happen to know someone who drives a teal Humber that's seen better days?"

Ron and Russell look at each other but stay silent. They don't want to drag their drummer into whatever it is they've somehow stumbled into.

"Well, whoever he is, we don't need company." Turning from the window, he shouts to the front: "Get rid of him!"

"There's a roundabout coming up," Archie answers. "I bet I can lose him there."

Rocco walks back toward the front of the van and sits down. His timing is perfect since, just a second later, the van jolts forward. Ron and Russell fall backward and roll onto the van's floor which, they discover, smells faintly of ammonia. They're jostled about more as the van violently turns one way and then the other. They hear the screeching of tires and honking.

Rocco calls out, "We good?"

Archie checks the mirrors.

"Yeah, we lost him."

"Fabulous." Rocco turns back to the brothers and then grabs for another cigarette. "Like I said, boys, settle in—it's going to be a while."

⊕

Dinky manages to stay with the van as it heads back over the Thames and winds its way through Dartford. Just south of Lewisham, there's a huge roundabout. Even though cars approach from all sides, merging and exiting, Dinky manages to stay behind the van. They're just about to pass the fourth exit when the van suddenly speeds up and veers wildly to the right.

"Goddamn it!" Dinky yells. "He's gonna make the turn!"

Dinky gives a quick glance over his shoulder and sees a silver Vauxhall blocking his way, an elderly woman with thick spectacles behind the wheel. He hits the brakes to let the Vauxhall pass so he can slip behind it and make the exit. His tires screech as the Vauxhall honks, slowing down as well and trapping Dinky in the lane.

"Bollocks," he yells again, unable to do anything but loop around one more time. From the opposite side of the roundabout, he gets a glance of the van as it retreats into the distance. Finally, the exit comes up again and he takes it, even though he knows it's hopeless. He speeds down the street, hoping to catch up to the kidnappers, but they're long gone. The van's either too far ahead or it's taken any number of turns on either side, streets heading off to all kinds of different destinations.

Dinky pulls off to the side of the road to decide what to do. He figures he can go back to the house in the suburbs, or he can finally go to the studio and tell Muff and the rest of the band what's happened. Figuring there's strength in numbers, he decides to head to the studio.

A half hour later, he arrives at Oxford Circus. AIR Studios, which was founded by Beatles producer George Martin, is located on the fourth floor of the Peter Robinson department store. Since it's now midday, the area's filled with cars and housewives with shopping bags. Dinky tries the National Car Parks on both Brewer Street and Dufours Place, but both are full. Cursing, he pulls into the garage on Harley Street, parks, and races through Cavendish Square. Crossing Regent Street, he's almost hit by a double-decker bus.

Dinky enters the Peter Robinson lobby and repeatedly presses the call button for the lift. Once he arrives at the fourth floor, he rushes past reception and into the control room of Studio Two. Muff's at the mixing desk. Through the glass, Dinky can see Trevor and Ian in the live room sitting on their amps and smoking. A rough mix of one of the new songs blares out of the speakers. The vocal and keyboards are just guide tracks, something for the rest of the band to play to. Ian and Trevor, seeing Dinky, smile and wave. Muff turns to see who they're waving to. When he sees it's the drummer, he sighs and looks at his watch.

"Fucking hell, Dinky, the day's half over! Where have you been? And where are Ron and Russell?"

Dinky spots a trio of brown bags sitting on top of a pile of Ampex tape boxes. The room smells like cheese and onions. He points.

"Is that food?"

"Yeah, sandwiches. The usual."

Dinky rushes over and opens each of the bags. He chooses the pressed veal and tomato.

"We got tired of waiting," Muff continues, "so we ordered without you."

As Dinky's inhaling the sandwich, Ian and Trevor enter the control room.

"Well, well," Ian says, laughing, "look who finally decided to show up."

Dinky ignores this, continuing to eat. Muff allows him a few more bites before trying to figure out what's going on.

"Where are the boys? What's happened?"

"Dunno," Dinky says, almost done with the sandwich. "I mean, I saw where they went, but I don't know where that is."

Muff shakes his head.

"You're not making a bit of sense. Why don't you start at the beginning?"

The drummer takes a few seconds to gather his thoughts.

"I went round to Ron and Russell's flat, like I do every morning. Only they weren't there."

"What time was this?"

Dinky thinks back.

"About eleven. Maybe a few past."

"Eleven?" Muff shouts. "You should have been here by then! You know this place is costing us forty-five pounds a day."

"I'm sorry," Dinky protests. "It's that damn construction on the M16. It was backed up all the way to Camberley. I sat there for over an hour."

"Forget that," Muff says. "Okay, you got to their flat. Then what happened?"

"I honked like I always do when they're not at the curb, which they usually ain't. Only they never came down."

"But you said you'd seen them."

"A few minutes after that, coming out of a hotel down the street. Only they weren't alone."

"Who was with them?" Trevor says. "Girls?"

"No," answers Dinky. "Couple of blokes. Three of them. Tough types, gangsters."

"And you're saying what," Muff says, "that Ron and Russell went somewhere with them?"

"Yeah, but not by their own choice."

Laughing again, Ian says, "What are you on about, Dinky? Are you winding us up?"

"I'm telling you fellas the truth! Three hard-looking geezers forced Ron and Russell into a car and then it sped away."

While Ian and Trevor trade skeptical glances, Muff asks, "What kind of car was it?"

"Rover, maroon. Pretty recent make."

Thinking this is all just another one of Dinky's outlandish excuses, Ian and Trevor go back into the studio. Through the glass, Dinky watches as they laugh and light up cigarettes.

"Muff, I'm telling the truth, I promise."

"I believe you, Dinky. But where did these guys take Ron and Russell?"

"Some house way out in Newham."

The producer ponders this for a second.

"That's hardly gangster territory. Okay, so you saw the boys taken inside the house. Then what happened?"

"Well, I just sat there."

"But what did you see?"

"Nothing. For over an hour no one went in, and no one came out."

"What about the men who took them?"

"They stayed outside."

"And where were you?"

Dinky grabs for the last bit of sandwich, takes a bite. Chewing, he says, "Down the road a ways. But they never saw me."

"So, they're still there?"

"No, 'bout a half hour ago some guys from inside the house wearing balaclavas came out with Ron and Russell, only the brothers were bound and gagged and tied together at the wrists."

"What, balaclavas? Dinky, are you sure?"

"Positive. They were practically carrying them since the brothers' legs were tied up. The guys with the masks had some quick words with the gangsters, then they shoved Ron and Russell into the back of a Commer and took off. I tried to follow but lost them at a roundabout. Then I came here."

Muff takes a deep sigh.

"If it was Roxy Music, I could see this happening. But Ron and Russell? I can't imagine how they could have made any enemies."

More laughter from the live room causes Dinky to look into the studio. This gives him an idea. Turning back to Muff, he asks, "Is Ade coming in today?"

"No, we're just doing basic tracks today. Adrian won't be in until Monday; why?"

"Because I want to go back out there."

"Out where?"

"The house. Newham."

"But why?"

"I don't know, to look for clues. Or maybe the boys will be brought back."

While Muff's weighing his options, Dinky continues.

"I'll take Ian and Trevor with me. They're strong blokes. If there's a punch-up, they'll be able to hold their own."

"Dinky, I don't know."

"We have to. Ron and Russell are out there somewhere,

and they need our help."

Muff finally says, "Okay, Dinky. But for God's sake, be careful."

2.
THE
SPEEDBOAT

Through the back window of the van Ron sees gray skies, green trees, and only the occasional electrical line or stoplight. They've been driving for almost two hours. The thugs up front are mostly silent, the radio turned down too low to be heard in the back. Rocco, lulled by the rhythmic rocking of the vehicle, fell asleep a while ago. His snoring is almost as loud as the van's engine. Not having come up with any good ideas on how to escape—their legs are a knot of cramps, and their hands are beginning to turn blue—Ron and Russell contemplate trying to take a nap too. They would, except the road is occasionally rough and the van jerks whenever it hits a bump. The brothers are light sleepers.

To pass the time, Russell thinks of the girl they met at the hotel that morning. He was planning on calling her for a date but, given where the day is heading, he doubts that's going to happen. It's probably for the best. He has a feeling that Ron likes her too. Women have always been a touchy subject between the brothers. Girls usually prefer Russell over Ron. Ron's too intense, too tall, a bit awkward. Russell's cute and cuddly, a teddy bear who also just happened to be on the football team. Growing up, when girls called the house, they usually wanted to talk to Russell. Things were going good for them in London, and he would hate to ruin that. Russell sighs with relief, knowing that death will get him out of having a difficult discussion with his brother.

As Ron sits there, looking up at the window, he figures that—if he was a different kind of writer—he'd turn all of this into a song. *Trapped in a van, baby, doing all I can . . . to get back to you.* But that's not who he is. Ron doesn't write from his life. His lyrics are fantasy or nonsense or fantastical nonsense. Stories he invents to make himself laugh. That's why he couldn't wait to get out of LA. All those Laurel Canyon songwriters baring their souls and refusing to take a shower made him sick. Ron doesn't feel he has anything to confess, and if he did, he wouldn't do it in a song.

The smell in the van gradually shifts from the aftershave and cigarette smoke to salt air and fish, a marginal improvement. Finally, Archie calls out, "Be there in just a minute, boss."

Rocco wakes up.

"All right, Archie, that's fab. Thank you." Shaking off sleep, he turns to the brothers. "I'm afraid you'll be leaving us soon."

"Who are you giving us to?" Ron asks, not sure he really wants an answer.

"An old mate of ours. His day job is smuggling, but for the right price he'll take on more specialized tasks. You'll like him. For as long as you know him, that is."

"You don't have to do this," Russell says.

"This ain't Hollywood, mate. We all have to make a living."

"We won't talk, I swear," Ron adds.

"I know you won't."

Rocco walks over on his knees and stuffs the gags once again into the mouths of the brothers. Ron and Russell are too weak to try and resist.

The van comes to a stop and Archie and Tommy hop out. A few seconds later, the back doors are opened. After the hours spent in the dark van, the hazy midday sunshine stings Russell's eyes and he quickly squints. Ron, still wearing sunglasses, doesn't react.

"End of the road for you lot."

Rocco gets out of the van, limping a bit due to a leg that had also fallen asleep. Archie and Tommy reach in and drag out the brothers. Ron and Russell uneasily stand, facing opposite directions.

The van is parked at the end of a dirt road that dead-ends into a makeshift dock tucked into a cove hemmed in on both sides by huge chalk cliffs. A weathered white speedboat is tied to the shore with a long piece of rope. A wooden pier that looks homemade extends about twenty feet into the water, the tied-up boat knocking into it rhythmically as it moves with the waves. The ocean beyond looks like a black cake with white frosting. The smuggler's sitting in the boat wearing a red knit cap and smoking a pipe. This is Des. He gets up when he sees the group approach. Des is older but more fit than the three gangsters; the brothers can see muscles underneath his tight, striped sweater.

"Hiya, Des," Rocco calls out, approaching the short pier. "How ya been?"

"Can't complain," Des calls back.

They meet on the shore and shake hands. Pointing to the brothers with a nod of his head, Rocco says, "These geezers shouldn't give you too much trouble."

Des steps forward to size up Ron and Russell as Archie and Tommy march the brothers from the dirt of the road to the water's edge. The shore is made from huge pebbles that shift every time the brothers take a step; it feels like they're walking on marbles. This is nothing like the beaches they grew up with in Southern California.

"These lads are rather posh. Quite a change from the yobbos you usually send me." The smuggler steps forward to examine the brothers more closely. Pointing to Ron, he says, "I reckon he's an accountant who got caught cooking the books. And him," he says, pointing to Russell, "he's a hairdresser in Sloane Square who slept with the boss's wife."

All four of them laugh. The brothers just stand there awkwardly.

"Load 'em in for me, boys," Des says. "I'll take it from there."

While Tommy and Archie are pushing the brothers forward, the smuggler asks Rocco, "Just the usual, or will you be wanting something special today?"

"Just the—" But he buckles over in a sneeze before he can continue.

ACHOO.

Once again, Rocco wipes his arm on his sleeve. "Sorry 'bout that—nah, just the usual if you please, Des."

The smuggler nods and follows Archie and Tommy down the short pier. Tommy gets into the boat to help the brothers in since they need to be lifted and placed into the speedboat at the same time, as if they were a mattress.

There's nothing to the speedboat besides a stand-alone chair for the driver and a long bench at the back. Otherwise, the whole center is empty except for two breeze blocks, some coiled rope, and a burlap bag.

"Yes, just place them back there; thank you, boys."

The brothers are placed onto a black leather bench seat with a white back. The wooden deck had been white at one time to match its fiberglass shell, only most of the paint has been worn away, showing the gray wood underneath.

Tommy jumps back onto the pier, and both he and Archie retreat to the van. Des and Rocco trade a few more words before the smuggler walks to the speedboat. He hops in and starts the engine. It chugs like a muscle car. He grabs the steering wheel, shifts into reverse, and—looking over his shoulder—begins to maneuver the boat out of the shallow cove.

The thugs stand on the shore and, even though the motor is loud, Ron and Russell hear Rocco call out as the speedboat slowly heads out to sea, "Bon voyage!"

Ian, sitting next to Dinky in the Humber, still doesn't believe it. Trevor's in the back seat, lying longways with his feet up and smoking a cigarette. They're almost to the house in the suburbs.

"Balaclavas, are you sure?" Ian asks for the third time.

"I'm telling you, mate, yes," Dinky insists, passing by a row of pubs on Green Street. "I know what I saw."

"You're saying these geezers were Provos?"

Dinky takes a sharp turn and answers, "Well, I doubt they were Paras."

Trevor finally speaks from the back seat.

"I had a cousin in the Parachute Regiment."

"Really?" Dinky finds the guitarist's eyes in the rearview mirror. "What happened to him?"

"Took a brick to the head one night outside of Divis Flats. Now he just sits around and watches *Mastermind*."

Ian whistles while Dinky concentrates on the road. They're just a block away.

"Okay, it's right up there."

Trevor sits up straight, leaning on the back of the front seat with his elbows.

"Which one?"

"The one with the tall hedge."

The scene is the same as how Dinky left it. The Rover's there; the van is gone. Curtains are drawn on the windows, so it's hard to see if anyone's inside or not.

Dinky doesn't want to park in the same space in case he'd been seen earlier by the goons in the van, so he drives past the house and makes a U-turn where the street begins to curve, heading up a hill. He parks on a side street. They have a clear view of the house over the lawn of a corner lot. When Dinky turns off the engine, the car shakes and knocks before coming to a rest. The smell of gasoline fills the interior.

"Jesus, Dinky," says Ian, rolling down the window, "your car's seen better days."

"I'll have you know this automobile has a proud history," Dinky declares. "In World War II, it was converted by the military into a reconnaissance vehicle."

"What," laughs Trevor, "this actual one?"

"You're both mad," Dinky protests over the laughter of his bandmates. "It's a collector's item—they stopped making them in the sixties."

"No wonder!"

When the laughter dies down, Ian and Trevor look at each other and then at Dinky.

"So then," Ian says, "what do we do now?"

Dinky's used to having eyes on him. As a drummer, he's the heart of the band. Dinky decides when to slow down a song or speed it up and, when he stops playing, the music comes to a halt. He's the glue, and he knows it. "It doesn't matter whose name is on the marquee," an old promoter friend from his cabaret days once told him. "*You're* the leader. Remember that."

Taking charge, he says, "Okay, this is what we're going to do. We sit tight until the van comes back. If Ron and Russell aren't in it, we'll just make them tell us where they are."

"The gangsters?" says Trevor. "Are you daft?"

"There's three of us and three of them," Dinky says. "You saying we can't take them?"

"It's not them I'm worried about," says Ian, nodding toward the house. "I don't want to mess with no mad bombers."

"He's winding us up, mate." Trevor points to the leafy trees and wide lawns. "Look around. All you're going to get out here are mad housewives."

"Don't be soft," says Dinky. "You know what they say, 'One bomb in London is worth thirty in Belfast.' This is war."

"I agree with Trevor," says Ian, nodding toward the rows of houses. "This doesn't look like war."

As Ian and Trevor continue to eye each other with skepticism, Dinky sees what needs to be done. He opens the car door.

"Look, I'll go and see what's happening, okay? Scope out the place. Maybe those other fellas have gone, and we can all go and have a proper look."

Trevor and Ian trade glances. They haven't been in the band very long, and so far Dinky's been a pretty quiet guy. This is impressing them.

"Okay, mate," Trevor says, "but be careful."

Dinky's getting out of the car when he stops and reaches over Ian to open the glove box.

"Might need a little disguise," he explains.

As he's grabbing one of the pairs of sunglasses he saw earlier, he touches the handle of the Derringer. He considers taking that too, just in case, but decides to leave it. He puts on the sunglasses. They're orange and see-through.

"That don't look suspicious at all," laughs Ian.

Dinky ignores this, gently closes the door of the Humber, and begins to walk toward the house.

When he's just a few yards away, a car turns onto the street from the main avenue and begins to head toward him. Dinky—wearing a white suit, blue shirt, and the orange sunglasses—looks awfully conspicuous, but the car passes. Dinky lets out a huge sigh.

He walks past the house but then cuts in, running across the lawn and entering the backyard from a side gate that's open. He closes it behind him, careful not to let the latch make a noise. The backyard is large and well-kempt. There's a bed of roses and a vegetable patch. A row of silver garbage bins is toward the back. Dinky considers going through them to see if they hold any clues, but there are two windows on the second floor with no shades and going through the trash would expose him. Instead, Dinky walks around the house as quietly as he can in his shoes that have a two-inch wooden heel.

Outside the dining room window, he hears voices. They're too quiet for him to make out words. He crouches by the window and tries to peer in, but all he sees is a brown duffel bag and several guns on a dark wood table. Swallowing hard, and pushing down fear, he continues walking along the stone path to the front of the house.

When he's close to the street, he hears another car but it's still not the van. It's a yellow sedan coming down from the hill toward town. Dinky pauses to let it pass. He's at the edge of the house now. The windows in the front are covered by drapes, but he figures he might be able to get a name off the mailbox, so he slowly creeps around. There's nothing on or near the front door that tells him who might live there, but as he's preparing to make a run back to the Humber, he sees something in one of the tall hedges that stand on either side of the front door. It's white and long and stuck low in the branches. Dinky walks toward the hedge and tugs at the item. In an instant, he knows what it is. He pulls it free, tucks it under his blazer, and sprints to his bandmates.

"What happened?" Ian asks before Dinky's even back in the car.

Without letting him answer, Trevor, leaning forward from the back seat, asks, "Did you see the bombers?"

Getting his breath back, Dinky answers, "I didn't see the men in masks or the bombs. But I heard voices, and I saw guns."

"Guns?" Ian says, his voice rising. "What kind of guns?"

"Rifles."

"Rifles don't mean nothing," chides Trevor. "I have plenty of mates who have guns for hunting, and they're not terrorists. They're barely hunters."

"Forget all that," says Dinky, speaking normal now that he has his breath back. "I found this."

He produces the item from inside his blazer.

Ian and Trevor don't need to look at it twice to know what it is.

"Christ," gasps Ian, "that's Russell's scarf."

"It ain't West Ham," Trevor says ruefully.

"Wh—what does this mean?"

"It means," Dinky says, "someone's nicked our songwriters."

"But what do we do?"

Dinky, clutching the scarf, looks back at the house and says, "We wait. Nobody steals somebody from my band and gets away with it."

The speedboat rushes toward the gray horizon going ninety miles an hour. Any sun from earlier in the day is gone, the sky filled with clouds black and heavy with rain. As choppy waves send the speedboat flying, Ron and Russell rise off the bench and float for a fraction of a second. Water splashing over the side dots Ron's slacks, and Russell's long hair is damp from the spray. Their thin sweaters are no match for the chilly salt air. Being in the van was preferable to this.

Ron twists his head and manages to look back to the shore, which is getting smaller and smaller every second. The cove they emerged from is lost in the various nooks and crannies of the rocky coast but, to the left, he sees a large town with a huge pier that extends far into the water. He can see what looks like hotels, cars, neon signs, and even ant-sized people going about their day.

The second-to-last show they'd played on their recent tour was in a seaside town. They'd performed for two thousand screaming kids at the Kursaal Ballroom in Southend-on-Sea. Since it was early July, the city was filled with vacationers with tans from wrist to neck. But that was only an hour outside London, and they drove twice as long today to get to wherever they just left, so Ron figures he's looking at a different town.

The smuggler suddenly begins to throw the speedboat

into a series of sharp turns. This causes the brothers to slide the length of the bench, shooting one way before being thrown seconds later in the other. After three or four turns, and almost falling overboard after each one, the brothers wonder if that's exactly the plan. By the time Ron has a chance to look back at the shore, it's gone. He now sees horizon in all directions.

Satisfied they've traveled far enough, Des kills the engine. The boat bobs up and down, tossed by the waves and the wake caused by the speedboat's various high-speed turns.

"I'm sure you think this is an unsavory way to make a living," Des says, rising from the steering wheel. He speaks loudly to be heard over the crashing ocean. "But people have been smuggling along this shore for centuries. Started with wool, believe it or not."

As he moves toward the breeze blocks, Ron and Russell stiffen. They imagine themselves sinking to the ocean floor, weighted down by the chunks of cement.

"Sure, it's shorter to get to France from Kent, but we still see a fair amount of traffic in these waters."

When Des reaches past the breeze blocks, opting instead for the burlap bag, the brothers are relieved. The smuggler pulls a shotgun out of the burlap bag. Ron and Russell wish he'd gone for the breeze blocks. Des quickly checks the barrels, making sure it's loaded. He snaps it shut and approaches the brothers.

Behind Des, a huge wave is forming. Whitecaps and

black ocean roll and swell. The wave is so big, it's liable to capsize the speedboat, sending them all to their doom. The brothers try to warn the smuggler, doing their best to speak through their tight gags, but all they manage are grunts. Des assumes they're begging for mercy.

"Sorry, lads, but there's no time for last requests." He raises the gun and shuts one eye, taking aim. "Nothing personal, boys. It's just business."

His finger's about to pull the trigger when the boat quickly rises, caught in the curve of the enormous wave. The smuggler loses his footing and is pitched forward, the speedboat almost vertical. He heads straight for Ron and Russell. Together, the brothers heave themselves to one side. Des hits the bench and rolls over the back of the boat, along with the shotgun, into the water. If he screams, the sound is lost to the roar of the sea.

As the boat crests over the wave, the brothers are thrown forward and find themselves face down on the deck. They slide under the dashboard before traveling the length of the boat and hitting the foot of the bench at the back. A few inches of water slosh around the deck. When they slide forward again, and are pushed up against the breeze blocks, Russell has an idea. He pulls his and Ron's hands over to one of the blocks. He can feel that the edge is sharp and rough-hewn.

As the boat continues to pitch and rotate, Russell runs their joined hands repeatedly over the breeze block, back and forth, back and forth. Ron, at first unsure what his brother's trying to do, finally understands and joins the effort. In just a few minutes, they manage to cut through the ropes.

They both reach up to the gags and untie them. The brothers gasp for air and exercise their jaws, spitting out bits of the cotton they'd chewed off. Ron quickly unties the ropes at his feet, despite his freezing hands. When Russell has trouble, his long hair in his eyes and the speedboat continuing to rise and fall on the waves, Ron reaches over to help. In a minute, they're both free. The sea finally calm, Russell walks carefully to the side of the boat and looks over.

"No sign of him," he says.

"That's good."

He turns to his brother.

"You don't think we should go after him?" Russell looks around. "Maybe there's a life preserver or something. He might still be alive."

"Russell, that guy was going to kill us. He was two seconds away from blowing our heads off. Why would we save him?"

"Seems like the nice thing to do." He looks out over the waves. It's just water in every direction. "He still might make it. I bet he's a good swimmer. People swim the English Channel all the time."

Ron walks to the front of the speedboat and examines the dashboard.

"No radio," he says. "No way to call for help."

Looking up at the sky, Russell says, "If we were sailors, we'd be able to tell how to get back to land by just looking at the stars."

"It's daytime."

"Then the sun."

Ron looks up.

"It's cloudy."

As they're standing there, trying to think of what to do, a wave lifts the speedboat. The brothers grab hold of the side and hang on. Ron sees, for barely a second, a glimpse of land. The pier, the town, the coast.

"The shore, I saw it!"

Russell looks around.

"Where?"

Ron jumps behind the wheel and starts the boat.

"Back there, on the right."

"On the right of what? We're spinning in circles."

"Just sit down and trust me."

The engine roars into life. Ron presses down on the accelerator. Russell flies to the back of the boat and barely catches the bench before going overboard and meeting the same fate as the smuggler. In just a few seconds, the coast is in view.

Trevor's out of cigarettes, and Ian keeps shifting uncomfortably in the seat of the Humber, kicking at the frayed green carpet at his feet. Even Dinky's bored. For the past hour, the three of them have just sat there, waiting for something to happen. Nothing has happened. A handful of cars have come and gone, driving lazily up and down the street, and a few people have emerged to walk a dog, but there's been no movement at the house with the hedge.

"Should we call the studio?" Ian suggests. "Muff might be worried."

"Not yet," Dinky replies. "We've nothing to tell him."

"But we could just check in. Maybe he's heard something," Trevor says from the back seat. "I saw a pub a way back. I bet they have a phone."

"You just want a pint, mate."

"So, what if I do?"

"We need to stay here, lads," Dinky announces. "We can't risk the kidnappers coming back while we're all at the pub playing darts."

"Trevor and I could go," suggests Ian, "and leave you here. You know, as a lookout."

"What happens if they come back and I need to follow them, but you two have the car?"

"We'll walk," says Trevor, sitting up. "The exercise would do us good—I've been cooped up all day."

"Yeah, and if something happens," adds Ian, "you can just swing by and pick us up."

"Don't be daft," says Dinky. "I can't take on all three of them on my own, now can I? We're going to stay right here and wait."

Ian and Trevor slump in their seats, disappointed.

A half hour later, the van comes back. Dinky spots it as soon as it turns onto the street.

"There it is!"

The van turns around and parks nose to nose with the Rover. The three thugs get out, each smoking a cigarette. Trevor leans forward and squints, examining the men.

"Yup," he says, "those fellas look like gangsters to me."

Ian sizes them up.

"Only one of them's big," he says. "The guy with the thing on his face. The other two are well small. I think Dinky's right. I think we can take 'em."

Thinking of a fight gets Trevor's blood going. He makes a fist and punches it into his palm. Maybe a bit of aggro is just what the day needs.

Instead of just standing around, like they had been before, the three goons go to the door of the house, knock, and are let inside.

"Where are Ron and Russell?" says Ian.

"You think they're still inside the van?" says Trevor.

"It's worth a look," says Dinky.

He's stepping out of the car when the front door of the house opens again. Dinky quickly gets back into the Humber.

Tommy goes to the back of the van and opens the double doors.

"Blast, it's empty," Dinky says, slapping the steering wheel.

Before he can say anything else, Liam and Shane—still wearing balaclavas—exit the house carrying brown duffel bags. The bags are placed in the back of the van.

"Fucking hell!" Ian says. "Dinky, you were right!"

Another duffel bag is carried out by Archie. Rocco and Quinn emerge from the house.

Inside the Humber, Trevor turns to Dinky.

"Sh—should we go to the police?"

Not taking his eyes off the back of the van, Dinky replies, "And tell them what? As we were searching for two skinny Americans—one of whom looks like Marc Bolan, while the other looks like Hitler—we found some IRA bombers hiding out in the suburbs? They'd never believe us. Hell, you two didn't believe me, and we're in the same band."

"So, then what do we do?" Ian says, looking back and forth from the van to Dinky.

The goons and the men from the house split up. The three thugs return to the Rover as Quinn gets behind the wheel of the van. Liam and Shane hop into the back of the van and close the doors from the inside.

Dinky turns the key in the ignition, the Humber spluttering to a start.

"We follow them."

The van pulls away first, the Rover quickly turning around and falling in behind. Dinky waits a few seconds before pulling away from the curb. Once they're in traffic, and driving through the small town, Dinky makes sure to remain a few car lengths behind. As they pass the pub they saw before, Trevor sighs.

"They're turning, they're turning!" Ian says, pointing.

"I see it," Dinky replies, making the same turn.

After they've gone a few miles, Trevor asks, "Where do you think they're headed?"

"I don't know," Dinky answers, "but this is different from where they went earlier."

"You think they're going to lead us to Ron and Russell?" Ian says.

"Maybe," Dinky answers. "All I know is that Ron and Russell aren't in that house, and they're not in the van. But those blokes up there know where they are."

After a few more miles, the cars separate. The van takes a turn while the Rover keeps going straight.

"What do we do?" says Ian anxiously. "Who do we follow?"

The Humber approaches the intersection, but Dinky can't make up his mind. The goons in the Rover are the ones who first took the brothers, but the van was the last place he saw them. Plus, the Commer has the weapons and the bombs. He jerks the wheel hard to the left.

"We're going to stick with the van."

They're halfway to London before Russell's done brushing sand off his pant legs. His wet socks sit next to him on the back seat of the burgundy Triumph. Ron, pressing himself into the door so he doesn't have to touch Russell's socks, looks out the window. The gray sky is reflected in the sunglasses he's been wearing all day. In the front are an artsy young couple they met near the pier in Brighton. The man's driving, the woman's dialing up a radio station. The brothers heard them talking about heading to Camden market to sell their wares, beaded jewelry and bracelets, mostly. Not having enough money for a cab to take them all the way into London, and thinking the train would take too long, Russell asked for a ride. The couple complied, even though they weren't quite sure what to make of the two men with the damp clothes and sandy shoes, one of which looks like a headmaster.

Russell turns to his brother and asks, "Did you really have to run the boat right onto the beach?"

Ron, not seeing any reason to try and find the cove where they'd first met the smuggler, decided to head straight for the big pier. As the speedboat got closer and closer, terrified swimmers paddled and ducked under the water to get away. Ron cut the engine when they were twenty yards from the shore. The boat coasted in, carried by the waves. The brothers jumped out, sinking into the soft sand. Russell was headed toward town when Ron called him back, convincing him they had to push the boat up higher. The waves were already beginning to draw it back out to the ocean. Ron was afraid it would break up against the pier or hit someone further down the beach. Russell grumbled but agreed, and together the two brothers waded back into the water and pushed the speedboat safely all the way onto the sand. Walking away, Ron turned to a sunburnt youth, pointed to the speedboat, and said, "It's yours." And now they're in the back seat of the Triumph, about to enter the city limits of London.

"You know what we need to do as soon as we're dropped off," says Ron.

"Change our clothes?" Russell suggests. "My pants are filthy and the shoes, I suspect, are a total loss."

"We need to go to the police and tell them what we know."

The radio starts playing "Radar Love." The woman turns it up, and the young couple bob their heads to the music.

"About the pub? Those guys said it was a hoax."

"No," Ron says, shaking his head. "About killing the Prince of Wales. I saw a bunch of guns as we were being led upstairs. They were in another one of those duffel bags."

Russell frowns.

"How do we know that isn't a hoax too?"

"I don't think we can take that chance."

Russell crosses his arms. He just wants to get to the

studio and put all of this behind them.

"Look," Ron continues, "if a member of royalty gets assassinated, and the tabloids find out that we knew about it beforehand, it's going to be a disaster."

Arms still crossed, Russell grudgingly replies, "I suppose so."

As the car begins to travel over the Thames, a new song comes on the radio. "Sugar Baby Love" by the Rubettes. Both Ron and Russell scowl.

"Honey, turn that off," says the driver. "I hate that song."

The brothers nod approvingly.

"I think we're getting close," whispers Ron. "Put your shoes and socks back on."

Russell pulls on the still-wet socks, grimacing.

After winding through a series of side streets, the Triumph pulls over and parks along a canal. Everyone gets out.

"Thanks for the ride," Ron says.

"Yeah, we really appreciate it," adds Russell.

The driver ignores them and goes to the trunk to get out the merchandise, while the girl smiles weakly and flashes the brothers a peace sign.

Backtracking to Camden High Street, Ron says, "I saw a police station a few blocks back."

Russell nods and follows.

After a few minutes, they find it. It's a square building sitting on the corner next to a butcher shop. Approaching the station, they see several posters in the window. One has two photos: a woman with a hat and a young boy in striped shirt and overalls. Above them, it says *Missing Persons*. WHERE ARE THEY NOW? Another poster features an unshaven man who glares at the camera. The huge type above reads £5,000 REWARD. ROBBERY AND DEATH OF OFFICER-IN-CHARGE.

The brothers enter the building just as an officer is leaving. The policeman's wearing an egg-shaped helmet with a strap that cuts right across the chin, trailing directly under his bottom lip. At first Russell figures they just didn't have the man's size when they were handing them out, but then, once they get inside the station, he sees they all fit like that.

There's a long and low wooden counter behind which are officers in uniform and plainclothes. A few of the policemen wear black military-style caps with a shiny plastic brim. They look better than the egg-shaped hats except for the black-and-white-checker rim that makes them look like cab drivers. Everyone's moving around hurriedly, barking orders into phones or consulting thick books, which Ron can see contain rows and rows of mean-looking faces.

A man behind the counter in a black uniform with three chevron stripes on the sleeve notices the brothers and steps forward.

"What's the problem?"

Russell looks to Ron to do the talking.

"Hello, Officer, we'd like to, ah—report a crime."

The man reaches for a pencil.

"Okay, what happened?"

"Well, it hasn't exactly happened yet. And we wanted to, you know, get you to stop it. From happening, I mean."

"Don't be clever with me, laddie," the officer says. "We only investigate crimes that have already happened. This ain't *Doctor Who*."

Seeing that Ron's not getting anywhere, Russell steps forward.

"Someone's going to assassinate the Prince of Wales."

"You're telling me someone wants to kill Prince Charles," the officer says skeptically, looking from Ron to Russell. "Next in line to the throne. What for, his ears being too big?"

"We don't know why," Ron says.

"Who told you this?"

"We don't know that either," adds Russell.

"Okay," the officer says slowly, closing his eyes. "Let me get this straight. You have information that someone's going to try and kill Prince Charles, but you don't know who's going to do it, and you don't know who told you this."

"That's correct," Ron says.

"Oh," interjects Russell, "and it's going to happen tonight at six."

The officer turns and looks to a round clock that sits high on the wall above a doorway.

"That's less than two hours from now."

"Well, then you'd better get going," Russell says.

The officer's face turns red. He licks the tip of the pencil and asks, "Right, what's your names, then?"

"Ron and Russell Mael," replies Ron. "We're in a band called Sparks."

"Never heard of you."

"We've had hit records. We were on television. *Top of the Pops. The Old Grey Whistle Test.*"

"I saw that," says a policeman in the back who's been eavesdropping. The brothers begin to beam with pride, until the officer adds, "Bob Harris said you was shite."

"Be that as it may," Ron says, clearing his throat, "we're on Island Records, and we're recording a new album at AIR Studios. In fact, we should be there right now."

"AIR Studios, you say?"

As Ron nods, and the officer's writing this down, another policeman appears. He's drinking a cup of tea.

"Americans, eh? You know, the *Evening Standard* notified us earlier about a tip they'd received of a bomb going off tonight at a pub near Harrods." He puts down the cup of tea. "We get reports like this all the time, and they usually check out. But this one was different."

"Wh-what was different about it?" Russell stammers.

"Well, the voice on the other end of the phone was an American." He turns to the man with the pencil. "Harry, where's the daily record book?"

Looking up from the pad of paper, he answers, "Bertie's got it. He's in the parade room."

The officer retreats. As they're waiting for him to return, the policeman with the pencil asks, his voice dripping with insinuation, "I hope you both know that calling in a phony bomb threat is a crime."

The brothers, beginning to get nervous, slowly back away from the counter.

"We should really get going," Ron says. "Thanks for the help, and good luck with . . . everything."

The officer notices them making their way toward the door.

"I think you boys should come on back here. We'll have a nice little chat."

Ron and Russell both break into a run. They're out the door in a flash. When they're halfway down the block, Russell looks back. Three policemen wearing the egg-shaped helmets are exiting the station, truncheons in hand and looking in all directions.

"This way," Ron says, taking a turn.

Still running, they backtrack the way they'd come earlier. Following a cobblestone road that overlooks a canal, they finally slow down. Russell checks behind them. The coast seems to be clear.

"I think we lost them," he says, out of breath.

Ron stops and sits on a small ledge overlooking the canal. He takes off his sunglasses to wipe the sweat from his forehead.

"That was close," he says, putting the sunglasses back on.

"Well, what do we do now?"

"We need to call the studio," Russell says. "Maybe Muff's heard something."

"Good idea," Ron says, hopping off the wall.

The red phone box smells strongly of urine. They all do, but this one stinks especially bad. Russell tries to stand outside of it, to make the call from the sidewalk, but the cord's not long enough. Instead, Ron keeps flapping the door back and forth, trying to get some fresh air into the small space. It's not working.

Russell fishes out of his pocket the piece of paper with the studio's phone number. He first sees Siobhán's handwriting. He quickly turns the paper over, puts in a few coins, and dials the number.

"AIR Studios, how can I help you?"

"Studio Two, please," Russell says quickly.

After a click and a few seconds, their producer answers.

"Muff!" Russell says. "It's Russell. How—"

"Where in the hell are you guys?" Muff cuts him off. "What's going on? The police just called. Did you threaten Prince Charles?"

"What, threaten? No. The, uh, police?"

"Yes, I just got off the phone with them. They said you'd been to the station, and you told them you were planning on assassinating Prince Charles. And when they tried to question you, you both took off."

"No, we were trying to warn—"

"But that's not all. They said you also phoned in a bomb threat. Chris Blackwell's not going to like this."

"Muff, please, let me explain. We didn't do any of that. Well, we did run away, and I did phone in about the bomb, but I was forced to! We were kidnapped this morning."

"So, Dinky was right?"

Russell suddenly remembers the guy in the van saying they were being followed by a Humber.

"What happened to Dinky?" Russell asks. "Is he okay?"

"I don't know, I haven't heard from him in hours. But he came in here around lunchtime with some cock-and-bull story about how, when he went to pick you guys up, he saw you get kidnapped and whisked away to some house in the suburbs."

"Yeah, yeah—that's exactly what happened. So, is Dinky there?"

"No, he's gone missing too! They all have."

"What do you mean? Who?"

"He took Trevor and Ian," Muff says, his voice heavy, "and they went out to look for you. That was hours ago now."

While Russell stands there, trying to process all of this, Ron stops with the door and asks, "What's happening?"

Russell looks up and says, "Now the band is missing."

"The band?" Ron gasps. "But we've just started working on the new album!"

"Will you forget about the album?" snaps Russell.

On the phone, Muff barks, "What's happening? Russell? Hello?!"

Russell turns his attention back to the phone.

"I'm still here. I'm just trying to process everything."

"Yeah, well, don't process anything here at the studio, because I have a feeling they were on their way over. And don't go home either. They asked for your address."

"Muff, why would you tell them that?"

"Look, Russell, you may be able to assassinate anyone you want in the United States, but here in England they take threats on the royal family very seriously. And when you combine that with bombing a pub, well, you know how many attacks there have been here in London. Why, just yesterday, at the Tower—"

Now Russell cuts him off.

"I know, I know. Anyway, we'd better go. We'll figure out something."

"Okay, call me back. And stay safe."

Russell hangs up the phone and exits the phone box.

Ron eagerly asks, "What'd he say?"

"We're fugitives. We can't go to the studio or back to the flat. The police are looking for us."

"Great. Now what?"

Russell leans against the phone box while Ron looks up

and down the street, eyes searching for policemen.

"We have to do something," Russell finally says. "If anything bad happens to Prince Charles, our career here's going to be over. We'll be on the first plane back to LA."

"Flying coach, no doubt."

Russell notices he's still holding the piece of paper. He turns it over and sees Siobhán's phone number.

"The girl!" he says, holding the paper for his brother to see.

"That's just great," Ron says, "we're about to be deported for regicide, and you're interested in a dame."

"No," Russell protests. "She works at a government agency, remember? The Department of Trade."

"So?"

"So maybe she can get a message through to someone. You know, notify those guys with the hats that look like Q-Tips. And they can warn Prince Charles. If we stop it, we won't get in any trouble."

"I don't know," Ron says.

"It's worth a try."

Russell moves to close the door of the phone box, but Ron places his foot in the path. The door remains half open. The brothers lock eyes.

"For the smell," Ron says.

Russell turns to the phone and dials. While it's ringing, he looks at the wall of the phone box. Every square inch is covered in graffiti. Above the placard housing instructions and local prefixes, someone's scrawled in huge block letters MARYLEBONE MARTYRS. *We hate everyone.*

A voice finally answers.

"Hello, Siobhán?"

"Yes, who's this?"

"Hi, it's Russell Mael. We met this morning at the hotel."

Down the street, Ron notices a policeman turn the corner and begin to walk toward them. Ron removes his foot from the door of the phone box and turns his back to the street, hiding his face and blocking the view of his brother inside.

The policeman gets closer and closer. Ron holds his breath. The man passes. Out of the corner of his eye, Ron sees the policeman reach the corner, turn, and continue walking.

He's letting out a huge sigh of relief when Russell emerges from inside the phone box.

"What did she say?"

"She's going to meet us at a restaurant in Soho in twenty minutes."

"Thank God," Ron says. "I'm starving."

It's a short cab ride to Flanagans, the pub near Regent's Park where Siobhán suggested they meet. The brothers choose a table in the front corner near a large window because a menu hanging from the red sign outside, underneath where the pub's name is spelled out in green neon, obscures the view. If Ron and Russell lean back, they can see around the menu and keep an eye on the street. If they lean forward, they're completely hidden and the table looks vacant.

The pub's dark and nearly empty. Only a few men drink solo at the bar while two waitresses stand near the kitchen, gossiping. A line of blinking fruit machines along the back wall provides the room's only light. The brothers nervously examine the menus as they wait for Siobhán.

"Can I get you gentlemen something?"

The brothers look to a waitress who suddenly appears holding a pencil and pad of paper. They're both starving, not having eaten anything since their meager breakfast. To stay incognito, Ron's still wearing his sunglasses, even though this makes reading the handwritten menu almost impossible.

"I'll have the, uh, let me see," he says slowly, holding the menu inches from his face. "I'll have the royal game pie."

"With spotted dick?"

"No, that's cleared up."

Confused, she turns to Russell.

"And for you?"

"Should I order a bunch of starters, in case Siobhán wants to have a bite too?"

Ron shrugs and looks to the street. Lots of people walk by the pub. None are policemen.

"Yes, then let me get an order of the tripe and onions," Russell says. "Some stewed eels, the cockles, the soused herring, and the chopped liver. No, make that jellied eels, instead."

"And to drink?"

"Just water, thanks."

The waitress rolls her eyes and says "tourists" under her breath as she retreats to the kitchen to put in the order.

While Ron keeps an eye on the street, Russell notices the bruises around his wrists from the ropes. He pulls down the sleeves of his sweater to hide the blue-and-purple marks.

"Here she comes," announces Ron.

They both look to the door as Siobhán comes bouncing into the pub carrying the white leatherette purse they saw her with that morning.

As she sits down, the waitress returns with the two waters for the brothers.

"Siobhán," Russell says, "would you care for a drink?"

"Oh, yes, please. I'll take a pink gin."

The waitress nods in acknowledgment and retreats once again.

"Sorry I'm late," Siobhán says, slightly out of breath. "I couldn't get a taxi, so I had to walk."

"It's no problem," Ron says. "Thanks for coming on such short notice."

"Happy to help." She turns to Russell. "What's so important? You sounded so mysterious on the phone."

"I'm sorry I couldn't tell you before." Russell keeps his voice low even though no one's around to overhear him. "It's just, the police are after us."

"Police? You two?" She laughs. "Don't tell me you skipped out on your breakfast this morning."

"We did, actually," says Ron. "But that's a different problem."

She looks confused, so Russell continues.

"Siobhán, we have reason to believe an attempt is going to be made on Prince Charles's life tonight at six o'clock."

She looks at her tiny wristwatch.

"That's in an hour."

"We know," adds Ron. "Can you help?"

"Help?" She looks from brother to brother. "What can I do?"

"You work at a government agency," Russell says. "The royal family's part of the government, right?"

The waitress returns with Siobhán's drink and sets it down. Siobhán takes a big sip.

"Yes, but . . . I told you, I'm just a secretary."

"Your boss perhaps," Ron suggests. "Maybe he would know how to get in touch with someone. The prime minister, maybe."

Not knowing what else to say, she takes another sip. A bigger one.

"We know this sounds crazy," Russell adds, "but it's true. You have to believe us."

"But what—how do you know this?"

"Right after we met you at the hotel this morning," Ron says, "three men kidnapped us. They tried to kill us—we only barely escaped—but before we did, we overheard their plan."

"They had guns," adds Russell.

"Are you sure?" Siobhán says. "This is England. People here don't have guns, not even the police."

"We know," Ron says. "We've been to see the police."

"And you told them what you know?"

"Yes," says Russell, "but they didn't believe us."

"So, they're not doing anything?" she says.

"No, which is why we thought of you. Can you help?"

She drains the last of her drink in a gulp.

"I can try, but I'll need to leave right now if I'm to catch my boss."

"You could call him from here," Russell suggests. "We'll wait. And we have food coming."

"No, I'd better just go."

She quickly opens her purse and pulls out the same black pen as before. Not seeing a piece of paper, she grabs Russell's left arm, pushes up his sweater, and begins writing.

"This is my phone number and address. Maybe you can come by later. I may have news." Done writing, she notices the bruises.

"You poor thing."

Ron quickly flashes his own bruised wrists and says,

"They tied me up too."

She's getting up when the waitress begins to deliver the appetizers.

"Goodbye, gentlemen," Siobhán says. "Wish me luck."

They stand up and watch her go. Russell sighs. When they sit back down, the table is covered in various small plates, bowls, and trays of food.

As the waitress is placing the last item, Russell points to a dish and asks, "Excuse me, miss, what's this one?"

"Your cockles, sir."

A half hour later, the brothers have eaten most of the food and the pub has slowly filled up. Outside, the streets are crowded. The offices are emptying and waves of commuters head for Euston Station a few blocks away. Some look for a place to have a drink and bite before traveling home. Every minute or so tourists stop to examine the pub's menu in the window near where the brothers sit. When they do, Ron and Russell lean forward and shield their faces.

"We should leave," Russell says.

Ron just nods and takes out his wallet. The bills are still a bit damp from the speedboat. He lays down a few pounds and they leave.

Once they're outside, Ron and Russell wish they were back inside. They feel even more exposed on the street. It's still light out, the midsummer sun breaking through the clouds a bit. Russell's white pants, finally dry, practically glow. The brothers walk briskly, looking around in all directions for the police.

After a block, they turn into a quiet mews. No one's around and only a few lights in the rows of carriage houses are on. They both exhale and relax their pace, walking slowly.

Russell asks, "Do you think it's going to work? That Siobhán's going to be able to help?"

Ron answers truthfully, "I don't know."

When they were kids, especially after their father died, Ron looked out for Russell. Protected him. If someone had a problem with Russell, they had to deal with Ron first. Russell was well-liked, never got into trouble, but there were a few occasions over the years when Ron had to step in and clear Russell's name. It's just what brothers do. But this is so far beyond what Ron's used to. Murder. Mad bombers. The police. It's all spiraled out of control, and Ron doesn't know how to handle it. He wonders if his days of protecting Russell are over.

"If things go bad, will we go back to Los Angeles?" Russell says.

Ron shakes his head.

"New York, maybe," he suggests. "We'll get some new guys. A new producer—a new label even if it comes to that. We'll be okay."

Russell's nodding when the mews ends and they turn

onto another street, one even busier than before. Women and men come at them from all directions. Cars stuck in traffic honk their horns and buses jam on breaks to avoid hitting jaywalkers. People are everywhere.

"We need to get off the street," Ron says.

Down the block, there's a pub. Russell points and begins to walk. Ron follows. As they get closer, the sign on the building comes into view. THE PRINCE OF WALES. The brothers stop walking. People bump into them, knocking Ron one way and Russell another.

Ron pulls Russell into the doorway of a store that's gone out of business.

"You saw that, right? The sign, the name of that place?"

"I did," answers Ron.

"You don't think—do you?"

"I don't know."

As Russell begins to nervously bite his lip, Ron sees a policeman in the reflection of the empty shop window. He's on the other side of the street, looking at the brothers.

"Come on," Ron says, pulling on Russell's sweater and dragging him back onto the sidewalk. They walk quickly to the Prince of Wales and enter.

It looks to them like any number of pubs they've been in since moving to England. The air is filled with smoke, and there's a portrait of the Queen behind the bar. The walls are covered in dark brown paint, and there's frosted glass everywhere. Men sit at tables nursing pints and playing dominoes. Toward the back, some dockworkers play darts, keeping score on a dusty chalkboard. The brothers find space toward the end of the bar and sit down.

"What'll it be, mate?"

"Two pints of bitter," says Ron, looking up just long enough to make eye contact with a young blond bartender, her hair pulled back. Neither of them drink, but he figures he'd better order something so they'll fit in. He fishes out more damp money and places it on the bar.

The bartender delivers the beers, scoops up the money, and moves on to serve another customer.

Under his breath, Russell asks, "What time is it?"

Ron looks at his watch.

"Five to six."

"Do you think this place is what those guys meant?"

Ron hates to have to keep repeating this—he's the older brother; he should have the answers—but he mumbles again, "I don't know."

"We should leave," Russell says. "This whole place could explode."

Ron looks to the entrance. The policeman he saw from before is standing outside the pub, looking in. He's speaking into a silver radio attached to his left shoulder.

"We can't; there's a cop right outside. It looks like he's calling for help."

"Well, maybe there's another way out."

Ron looks for a rear exit. At the far end of the pub,

underneath a sign reading *Gents Cloaks Stag Room*, there's a set of stairs heading down. Standing next to the stairs is a man with red hair who looks vaguely familiar. Ron takes off his sunglasses for a better look.

"That man," he says, elbowing Russell and pointing. "Do you see him?"

Russell scans the crowd.

"Who? What man?"

"That guy standing near the stairs. With the red hair. I've seen him before."

"When?"

"Christmas," Ron says. "The World's End. That pub near the practice space that got destroyed."

"What about it?"

"He was leaving the scene, after the blast. He walked right by me."

The man finishes his drink, looks around surreptitiously, and begins to walk quickly down the steps.

Ron and Russell rush to the top of the stairs just as the red-haired man turns and disappears down a dim hallway. The last thing Ron sees are the man's green shoes. He's just about to follow when Ron's stopped by a hand on his shoulder. The brothers turn around and see the policeman who'd been outside a few moments before.

"Pardon me, sirs, but I'm afraid I'm going to have to ask you both to come with me."

"That man," Ron shouts and points, "he's getting away!"

The policeman pulls them from the top of the stairs and begins to march them through the crowded pub back toward the street.

"You can tell me all about it at the station."

"You don't understand," Russell says as he's shoved toward the entrance. "There's a bomb; we need to warn people!"

"I'll give *you* a warning, laddie—button your lip, or I'll do it for you!"

The brothers exchange a brief glance and then wrestle free from the grip of the policeman. He gets out his truncheon but, by the time it comes down, it only grazes Ron's shoulder.

"Stop!" he calls out. But the policeman's command is drowned out by the blast of the bomb. Ron and Russell see red and fly through the air.

3.
THE
PETROL
STATION

R on and Russell hit the sidewalk like sacks of dirt. They lie there for a few minutes, only faintly aware of the commotion going on around them. Cars halt and drivers get out. Commuters stop and gawk. Many of the onlookers are made mute by the violence. They just stare in shock. Others are already angry and ready to cast blame. "Bloody Irish murderers," a woman clutching a bag of groceries to her chest says. "They should all be shot." Passengers from a stopped bus rush into the pub to save people, even the bus driver joins in. Those inside the pub who can walk on their own limp to safety. Others must be carried. Some don't move at all.

As Ron comes to, his ears are ringing. The monotonous, even sound is not unlike the dial tone he heard earlier in the day at the house in the suburbs, except now it feels like it's coming from inside his head. It's the only thing he can hear.

He begins to panic. He's a musician, a songwriter. He needs to be able to hear other sounds. How many tunes can he come up with that have just this one note?

Slowly, other sounds return, along with the sensation that he's being shaken. He thinks it's an earthquake, but it's just his brother. Russell has his hands on Ron's shoulders, and he's moving him back and forth. The sunglasses, already askew, now dance around Ron's face. Russell's voice does battle with the dial tone, but finally wins.

"Ron, can you hear me? Ron, look at me! Ron, are you okay?"

"Yes, yeah—at least, I think so."

Ron stands up and pats himself down, as if to make sure he still has arms and legs.

"I'm okay. How about you?"

Russell nods. Their clothes are dirty from hitting the ground, but otherwise the blast of the bomb that sent them flying also saved their lives. They were outside the building when it came crashing down.

They look to the pub's entrance and see the policeman trapped under the lintel. The man's hat has been knocked off, and he's bleeding from a cut on his forehead. Together and with some effort, the brothers manage to lift the huge chunk of wood off the policeman's back. They drag him out of the rubble and onto the sidewalk. Russell bends down to listen at the man's chest.

"He's alive."

The brothers are about to head back into the pub when they hear sirens. They turn, hoping to see the blue flashing lights of an ambulance, but instead they spot police cars. This must be the backup the policeman who'd collared them was requesting.

"We have to leave," Ron says.

Russell points to the gaping wound of fire and broken glass that stands where the pub used to be.

"We need to help people."

Ron grabs his brother by the elbow and begins to push him down the street.

"We can't do any good if we're in jail. They think we did this, remember?"

Russell looks back and sees the officers rush into the damage.

The brothers backtrack the way they came before, turning at the corner and entering the mews. The sky's now pink, the sun has disappeared, and lights appear in the windows. Ron and Russell keep their heads down, concentrating on the cobblestones.

They're just about to exit the small street when a car blocks their way. The engine idles menacingly. The brothers consider breaking into a run and turning back, except in that direction is the burning pub and the police. Forward is the only option. They both take a deep breath and slowly raise their eyes. They see the teal Humber.

"Dinky!"

Their drummer steps out of the car.

"Fellas!"

Ian and Trevor also get out. They size up the brothers and grimace.

"What've you boys been up to all day," asks Ian, "rolling around in the dirt?"

The brothers ignore this and focus on Dinky.

"How did you find us?"

"Well, after I seen you taken this morning, I tried to follow you—when you were in the van—but those mean-looking bastards gave me the slip. So I went back to the studio and got this lot. We returned to the house and followed the van again. Trailed them all the way out to Bromley. Took ages."

Ron hears something behind him. He looks down the small, curved street, but it must have just been footsteps headed toward the pub. More people trying to help.

Russell asks, "What did they do in Bromley?"

"Your friends in the ski masks picked up some red-haired fella."

"Did he have green shoes?" asks Ron.

"Aye, he did," Dinky says, surprised. "How'd you know?"

"We just saw him. He bombed that pub back there."

"Well, the van's parked a few blocks from here, only no one's in it. We got caught at a light and must have missed them getting out."

"Can you take us to it?" says Russell.

Dinky grins and says, "Get in."

It's a tight fit with all five of them in the sedan. Ian keeps his seat up front, while Trevor is sandwiched between Ron and Russell.

"You really wouldn't believe the day we've had," says Ron.

Dinky turns onto Hampstead Road. The smoldering pub is a block behind them.

Trevor says, "It ain't over yet, mate."

Dinky guides the Humber to a corner of Russell Square that's right across from the British Museum. He pulls alongside a large gap between a sports car and a sedan the same size as the Humber. Dinky kills the engine, the Humber sputtering and shaking before finally turning off.

Dinky slams on the steering wheel and shouts, "Bollocks!"

Ian adds, "They're gone."

"This is where the van had been?" says Russell. "You're sure?"

"This is where it was," confirms Trevor. "We all saw it."

"And there was nothing inside?" says Ron.

"Nothing," answers Ian. "The doors were locked, but we looked through the windows in the back. It was empty."

Dinky slams on the steering wheel again.

The five of them are sitting there wondering what to do next when a police car drives by. The car stops at the corner, sits there for a few seconds, and backs up. An officer gets out and begins to approach the Humber.

"Keep calm, lads," Dinky says, himself calm. "Let me do

the talking."

As the officer's just a few feet away, Dinky rolls down the window and sticks his head out.

"Evening, Officer!"

"Everything okay, son?"

"Just a spot of car trouble. Engine was overheating. We was just letting it cool down."

The officer bends at the waist and looks into the car. He examines the band, his gaze traveling from face to face. He lingers on Ron, not liking the look of his mustache, or the fact that he's wearing sunglasses when there's no sun.

"Let's look under the bonnet," the officer finally says.

Instead, Dinky starts the car. The Humber shakes violently, the engine taking a few seconds to catch, but it finally starts.

"Ah, well, will you look at that?" Dinky says. "I think we're fine now, sir. Thank you, Officer, for your concern. But we'll be on our way."

Even though the policeman is still staring at them, Dinky slowly pulls away. Russell looks back and sees the officer standing in the street, his eyes glued to the Humber. Dinky turns a corner. The policeman doesn't follow them.

"That was close," Ian says, letting out a lungful of breath.

"Aye, but I wasn't lying." Dinky points to a series of dials and gauges set into the dashboard. "This thing's been overheating all day."

"Your car's a hunk of junk," Trevor says, punching the

back of the front seat with his fist.

"Easy, mate," Dinky says. "Just need to find a petrol station, that's all. It probably just needs some water."

After driving a few blocks, Ian points to something in the distance.

"There, on the next corner."

"What?"

"Petrol station," Ian says. "Heron, see it? Pull in there."

A bright yellow Ford Cortina is just pulling out when Dinky and the band pull in. An attendant wearing a white smock over black overalls finishes replacing a gas nozzle into a pump and walks to the window of the Humber. Dinky turns off the car.

"You have a mechanic on duty?"

"I'm a mechanic, sir. What's the problem?"

From the back seat, Trevor says, "Car's a piece of junk, mate; that's the problem."

Dinky ignores this and gets out of the car.

"It's been overheating all day."

Popping the hood, the attendant says, "Let's have a look."

The attendant proceeds to examine the engine from various angles. He pokes at tubes with the tip of a tire pressure gauge and briefly gets on his back to look underneath the car.

"Ain't you going to check the radiator?" Dinky says,

pointing to where steam is escaping from around the edge of the rusted cap.

"And burn my face off? No, I'm going to let that sit for a few minutes."

"Minutes? Look, mate, we're in a hurry."

"I'm sorry, sir, but it could be any number of things."

"Like what?"

The attendant gets up off the ground and goes back to looking at the engine.

"Well, for starters, it might be the cooling fan, or a broken fan belt. The pipes may be clogged. The thermostat might be shot. Or your seams might be blown. I need some time to have a look around."

"Okay, but hurry up."

Dinky opens one of the back doors and says, "It's going to be a while, lads. You might as well stretch your legs."

Everyone gets out of the Humber. As Ian leans against a yellow column with a poster that says, *Fabulous Free Gifts* WITH HERON GOLD STAMPS *Cash Only*, Trevor gets out a pack of cigarettes. He lights one and takes a drag and then hands the pack to Ian. The attendant shoots him a look.

"Don't worry, mate," Trevor says. "We'll be careful."

Dinky approaches the brothers.

"How are you guys feeling? You okay?"

Russell tries to brush the soot and dirt from his pants, which are now off-white.

"We're okay," Ron says, looking toward the street. "I just

feel exposed standing out here."

"It won't be long," Dinky says. "But what's our next move? Where do we go from here? I doubt Muff's still at the studio."

"We can't go to the studio," Russell says. "Or to our apartment."

"Why not?" Dinky says.

"We're wanted by the police."

Ian approaches.

"You can stay at my gaff. It's not far from here."

"Thanks," says Ron, "but until we get this sorted out, I don't want to put any of you in that kind of danger."

"You need to sleep somewhere," says Dinky.

"Just drop us at a hotel. In the morning we'll call our manager and he'll help us sort it all out."

Everyone nods; that seems like a good idea.

As Trevor and Ian finish their cigarettes and light new ones, Russell pushes up the sleeves of his sweater. He sees the address and phone number written on his arm.

"Siobhán," he says.

"Who?" says Dinky.

Ron steps forward and asks, "What about her?"

"We should call her."

"Why?"

"We sent her on that wild goose chase. Prince Charles, remember? The assassination attempt?"

"What about it? We were wrong; it was a pub, not a

person."

"But we told her to go to her boss. What if she did and then got into some kind of trouble, thinking it was a prank?"

"Maybe you're right." Ron steps toward the front of the car and calls out to the attendant. "Excuse me, do you have a phone?"

He answers, his voice muffled by the raised hood, "Yeah, but it's busted."

"Maybe we can just stop by after the car's fixed." Russell shows Dinky his arm. "Do you know this address?"

Dinky cocks his head to be able to read the writing.

"Cazenove Road. That's in Stoke Newington."

"Is it far?"

"Not bad. Twenty minutes probably. Maybe less."

"Okay," says Russell, "when the car's fixed, you can drop us there."

"A bird," Trevor says, flinging the butt of the cigarette into the street. "It figures."

⁕

A half hour later, the attendant pulls his head out from under the hood of the Humber and waves Dinky over.

"Okay, sir, I've given the engine a thorough inspection. You need a bunch of things."

"Like what?"

"Your water pump's failing, and your hoses are leaking

all over the place. Plus, it's just a matter of time before—"

"Look, what can you fix fast? I told you, we're in a hurry."

The attendant looks from Dinky back to the car, weighing the options.

"Well, as a bare minimum I can just top you off with coolant and patch some of the leaks, but that won't last very long. The whole cooling system needs to be replaced, and if you don't get a new radiator soon, you're going to be looking for a whole new car."

"Fine, fine. How long will it take you to do that other stuff? And what kind of price am I looking at?"

"I can probably get you back on the road in about ten minutes. And it'll cost you five pounds."

"Get it done in half that and I'll give you a tenner."

"Yes, sir!"

As the attendant's about to return to work, Trevor notices a silver Jaguar parked next to the pumps. No one's inside, and it's been parked since they got there. He points and says, "This geezer in the loo, or what?"

"No, that's my car," the attendant says proudly. "The boss lets me park it there and work on it in between customers. It gets pretty quiet out here once rush hour is over."

"Our car." Dinky points. "Come on, chop chop."

The attendant runs into a small office located under a sign that says AUTO SHOP. He quickly hustles back to the Humber with a few spare parts under his arm.

Dinky approaches Ron and Russell, who are both leaning

against the trunk.

"Why don't you guys wait in the car. We'll only be a few more minutes."

The brothers think this is a good idea, so they get into the back seat.

The doors to the Humber are just closing when headlights rake the petrol station as a car turns in from the street.

"Looks like you have another customer," says Ian.

The attendant pulls his head out from under the hood and shouts, "Be with you gentlemen in a minute!"

The car pulls up behind the Humber. The headlights are still on. The bandmates shield their eyes from the glare. They hear car doors opening and closing, footsteps landing on the cement as whoever's inside the car gets out.

ACHOO.

The car's headlights go dark. It's the maroon Rover. Archie and Tommy stand there as Rocco once more wipes his nose on a sleeve.

"Well, well," he says, "what do we have here?"

He peers into the back of the Humber. Ron and Russell look to see what's happening. When they spot Rocco, the brothers turn their heads around so fast it almost gives them whiplash.

"Don't tell me there was a change of plans," Rocco says. "Those geezers were meant to be done for."

Trevor and Ian trade glances as Dinky steps forward.

"We nicked 'em. Turns out they're a famous band. Ought

to be worth a few thousand quid."

"I knew it!" Rocco turns to Tommy and Archie. "That's what we should have done, boys. Didn't I tell you?"

He turns back to Dinky and says, "Well, good luck to ya, I suppose. But you'd better tie them up or something. They're more clever than they look."

Dinky walks back to the Humber and ducks his head into the car. He spots Russell's white scarf sitting on the front passenger seat. "Ian," he calls out, "come give me a hand."

Dinky begins to rip the scarf into strips.

"Hey," Russell protests. "I bought that at Marks and Spencer!"

"Will you shut it?" Dinky says. "If we make it out of this alive, Island Records will buy you a new one."

Ian joins them, and Dinky hands him half the scarf. In just a few minutes, Dinky and Ian have ripped enough strips to fashion gags for Ron and Russell as well as to bind their hands together behind their backs.

"Okay," Dinky whispers to the brothers, "make these geezers believe it. Remember, we're your kidnappers."

Ron and Russell manage to turn themselves around in the small space and stick their heads into the back window of the Humber. They cock their heads left and right and move their mouths, pretending that they're struggling and pleading for help.

"Good," Dinky says, "keep it up."

Ian and Dinky pull their heads out of the Humber and join Trevor, who's having a staring contest with all three goons.

"Well, it looks like you've got it all sorted out," Rocco says. "We'll let you get on with it."

All three of them get back into the Rover, Archie once again behind the wheel. The maroon car slowly backs out of the petrol station and turns into traffic. No one in the band breathes until the Rover is out of sight.

"Bloody hell," says Trevor, "I can't believe that worked!"

Dinky leans back into the car and says to the brothers, "Best to leave you like this in case they come back."

Ron and Russell genuinely try to protest, squirming and trying to get Dinky to let them go, only their words are just grunts.

"That's perfect, lads, keep it up."

Dinky picks up what's left of Russell's scarf. As he's putting the pieces in the glove box, he sees the two pairs of sunglasses and pulls them out. He's closing the glove box when he remembers the Derringer. He takes it and quickly puts it in the pocket of his blazer.

Trevor and Ian are standing in front of the gas pump next to the Humber. Ian's holding a white paper cup.

"Where'd you get that?" Dinky says.

"It's tea," Ian says. "There's a machine back by the gents."

Dinky puts on the yellow sunglasses and hands the other ones to Ian.

"What do I need these for?"

"It'll help you look tough."

As Ian puts them on, he nods toward Trevor.

"Why doesn't he need them?"

"Trevor already looks tough."

"Almost done, sir."

Dinky turns and sees the attendant holding a faded green watering can.

"Just need to fill the radiator, then you'll be good to go."

"Fantastic. Hurry it up."

As Dinky leans against the Humber, Ian sips his tea and Trevor lights another cigarette. The attendant leans over the engine while the brothers continue to mutely peer out the back window.

A minute later, the Rover returns. The three gangsters get out of the car slowly.

"So," Rocco says, approaching the Humber, "you and Des was in on it, were you?"

"Des?" answers Dinky with a sneer.

"The smuggler. That's who you must have gotten those Yanks from. Because when we last saw them, Des was in a speedboat heading toward the horizon with orders to drop those two blokes in the middle of the channel."

Ian and Trevor look to Dinky. In the car, the brothers turn their heads to look at him too. The voices from outside are muffled but can still be heard inside the Humber.

"Des had a change of heart and phoned me up," Dinky

bluffs. "We go way back, we do."

"So, Des is smuggling people now? Our employers won't like that one bit. He was meant to do a job, and if those two in the car are still breathing, then that means he ain't done it."

"Well, then, you'd better take that up with Des."

Rocco looks back at Tommy and Archie and all three break out into laughter.

"What am I, some chump with a stump?" Rocco suddenly stops laughing. "You fellas ain't no gangsters. You're friends of theirs. We was half a block away when I remembered. We saw you before, in this car. You was following us."

When Dinky answers, he sounds less sure of himself than he did before. "I—I don't know what you're talking about."

"Look, let's stop pissing about. We're taking those two back, and you're not going to stop us."

Trevor steps forward and whispers into Dinky's ear, "There's three of them and three of us. We can handle 'em, I'm telling you."

"Take it easy," Dinky whispers back. "I've got an idea."

He steps forward and points to the car parked next to the Humber.

"You see this Jaguar? It belongs to our mates. They're in the toilet and will be out in just a minute. There's four of them. That makes it seven to three."

"Your friends are all in the toilet," Archie says, "together?"

"They went in there to reload. We pulled a bit of a heist earlier today."

Stifling a laugh, Rocco asks, "You're telling me you fellas have shooters?"

"That's what I'm telling you."

"I don't believe you. And even if you did, you'd never use 'em. You haven't got the guts of a flea."

Dinky pulls from his white blazer the Derringer. Leveling it at the three gangsters, he says, "Wanna bet?"

As everyone stands there—even the attendant has pulled his head out from under the hood and is transfixed by what's going on—time seems to stop. Even the cars passing by on the road next to the petrol station seem to go by in slow motion. Ron and Russell think back to all the double features they saw as kids when their dad took them to the movies. Every Western had a scene like this. A showdown. Ron even wrote a song about it.

When Rocco begins to reach into his blazer, Dinky fires two shots. One pierces the front of the Rover and the other lands right in the middle of Archie's shin. He instantly hits the ground, red blood making the pant leg of his dark blue slacks even darker. Meanwhile, steam hisses out the front grill of the Rover.

"All right, all right," Rocco says, hands raised in surrender. "We're going. We didn't know you was a hard nut."

This time Tommy gets behind the wheel as Rocco pulls Archie into the back seat. After the car drives quickly away from the petrol station, the dark pool of the gangster's blood blends in easily with the various oil and gas stains on the concrete.

As Trevor rushes to untie the brothers, Dinky puts the Derringer back into his pocket and says, "I'm really glad they left."

Wiping nervous sweat from his forehead, Ian asks, "Why?"

"I only had the two bullets."

On the way to Stoke Newington, Dinky can barely keep his mind on the road. He just shot a man and a car. He's not sure which to be more worried about. The man will live; the injury may have been painful, but it was minor. But the Rover—that's an expensive car. If they somehow find Dinky and make him pay for the repairs, he'll have to go to the label and ask for an advance. He's surprised he hit anything at all. He was aiming for the ground, like they do in the movies. Dirt flies around the bad guy's cowboy boots, and that's enough to end the fight. But as Dinky thinks about it now, he's glad he hit the car and the man. He read once that petrol stations store gasoline in huge tanks underground. If either of his bullets had pierced the cement, and entered one of the tanks, there would have been an explosion and fireball visible to half of London. The whole band would be dead. Plus, the Humber would have been totaled. Thinking of this makes him shiver. He loves this car.

In the back seat, Ron and Russell watch the streets go by in a daze. Trevor and Ian don't say much either. No one really knows what to think. Guns, bombs, gangsters. It certainly wasn't a typical Thursday.

"We're coming up on Cazenove Road," Dinky announces. "What was the address again?"

Russell pushes up his sleeve and tries to read Siobhán's writing in the passing streetlights.

"Cedra Court. Flat 1A."

Dinky nods and turns. He knows where that is.

The street contains row after row of terraced houses with low windows and narrow doorways. The sidewalks are mostly empty, even though it's only eight o'clock. A few people return home from dinner or drinks, and one or two are walking a dog, but otherwise the street is silent. The modest homes soon give way to big apartment buildings with names written on the outside. AVENUE HOUSE. HADLEY COURT. Right before the street dead-ends into Upper Clapton Road, they arrive at Siobhán's address. It's a huge art deco complex with a four-story building forming a horseshoe around an inner courtyard containing an expanse of grass surrounded by tall shrubs. The units with balconies have clotheslines strung across them, the clothespins looking like birds on a wire.

"Okay, boys," Dinky says as he pulls to the curb, "here we are."

Russell starts to get out of the car but stops.

"Dinky, we can't thank you enough for what you did back there."

"Yeah," Ron says, "we wouldn't be alive if it weren't for you."

Dinky shrugs and says, nonchalantly, "All in a day's work, mates."

Ron and Russell get out of the car.

"See you at the studio tomorrow," Ian says through the rolled-down window.

The Humber rattles its way to the corner, turns, and is soon out of sight.

Siobhán's apartment turns out to be a basement flat located behind the far corner of the horseshoe. It's across from an alley that runs the length of the building and, beyond that, is a huge parking lot. A short set of stairs behind a wrought-iron gate and railing leads to a white door. The gate opens with a creak. As Ron and Russell walk down the stairs, they can see Siobhán on the couch, legs folded beneath her, reading an issue of *Petticoat* magazine. The window is open, and they hear Charlie Parker playing softly on the radio.

Russell leads the way down the stairs and gives a short knock. Siobhán answers, holding the copy of *Petticoat*. Ron cocks his head and reads one of the cover's headlines. FASHION FOR FUN: *Who Wears Short Shorts?*

She's changed her clothes from when they saw her earlier in the day. Her work attire has been replaced with cream-colored capri pants and a dark blue sleeveless top with big white buttons and a Peter Pan collar.

"Well, hello, soldier boys."

"Hi."

"Hi."

When neither brother says anything else, she says, "Well, don't just stand there. Come on in."

She steps aside, and the brothers enter tentatively.

It's a small apartment, with a kitchenette along the back wall overlooking the alley and an open door exposing a bedroom. A coat rack holds several hats, coats, and umbrellas. The radio playing jazz sits on the windowsill, the antenna pointed toward the courtyard for the best signal. House plants hang from the ceiling suspended in macramé pot holders. The coffee table is filled with fashion magazines. Two rattan chairs sit opposite a low sofa. Above the sofa is a big painting of triangles and splashes of color.

Siobhán motions to the couch. "Have a seat."

The brothers sit down. The sofa, covered with an afghan, is old but comfortable.

Ron takes off his sunglasses and, since the small apartment is stuffy, Russell unzips his sweater. The room is dimly lit so his white pants merely look cream-colored— matching hers—rather than covered with dirt.

Pointing to the kitchen, she says, "Care for a drink?"

"No thanks," Ron says. "We don't drink."

When she sits down in one of the rattan chairs and

crosses her legs, the brothers can see that her toenails are painted bright red.

"Look, Siobhán," Russell says, "we just came by to say we're sorry."

"Sorry?" she says, surprised. "For what?"

"For sending you on that wild goose chase earlier today," Ron explains. "We hope it didn't get you into any trouble."

"We didn't do it as a prank," adds Russell. "I swear."

She reaches for a pack of Viceroys sitting on the coffee table and takes out a cigarette. Ron and Russell both search their pockets, but neither has a lighter. Ron finds only sand, and Russell pulls out a seashell.

Siobhán smiles at their effort. The brothers like her smile.

"Oh, *that*. Don't worry about it."

"It's no problem?" Ron says. "Your boss won't get mad?"

She takes a drag on the cigarette.

"It's fine, believe me."

Ron looks around the apartment for a phone.

"We could call him if that would help. Explain what happened."

"Seriously, forget it." She taps the cigarette against an ashtray. "Better safe than sorry, right?"

Both brothers nod, relieved.

Trying to make conversation, Russell asks, "This is a nice place. Lived here long?"

"Few years. I'd prefer something aboveground, but London's expensive." She takes a last drag on the cigarette and then stubs it out in the ashtray. "I'm actually glad you both came by."

"You are?"

"Yes. Like I said this morning, I find Americans fascinating."

Ron and Russell lean back on the couch, beaming.

"Tell you what." She gives a quick glance to her bedroom. "I'm going to take a quick shower and slip into something a bit more comfortable. How does that sound?"

The brothers are too shocked to speak.

Before getting up, she leans forward and places a hand on one of their knees. Giving a squeeze, she says, "You know, I've never had brothers before."

Siobhán winks and leaves the room. A minute later, they can hear a shower through the shut bedroom door.

Russell turns to Ron.

"What do we do?"

"I'm open-minded to the concept, but not—with you."

"Yeah, I mean, I like her but that feels like too much."

"I agree. One of us should go."

"But who?"

"There's got to be a million girls like her," Ron says and stops, quickly adding, "though I can't think of one."

This had happened before, though not since they'd left LA. Neither had seriously dated anyone since moving to London. There hadn't been any time. When they first arrived, Ron and Russell had been consumed with forming the band and writing a new batch of songs. The songs then had to be recorded. The album was released and, somehow, was a smash. They played shows. Girls screamed. The only problem was that the women were all too young. These weren't people they could have an affair with much less a relationship. There had been a journalist or two in England who'd flirted with them. That would have been okay. The problem is that the brothers were always together—they never did interviews alone. So there was never a case where Ron met a girl or Russell met a girl; they always met the same girl. And now it had happened again.

Ron finally says, "I'll go."

"Are you sure?"

"Yes. We've already been on a bed together once today. I don't need to do it again."

He's getting up to leave when, through the window, he sees someone walking through the courtyard. Ron pauses, waiting for the person to pass, but the shadowy figure is heading toward the basement apartment.

"Someone's coming."

The iron gate at the top of the stairs creaks as it's opened and shut. The brothers see a pair of green shoes and a brown duffel bag descend the stone steps. They get up quickly from the couch and run toward the back of the flat, searching for an exit. There isn't one. Russell's trying to frantically open the window above the sink when someone begins to knock on the basement door.

The knocking gets louder and louder as Russell's still trying to break the seal where the window's been painted shut, but it's no use.

Ron whispers, "He must have followed us here."

From the bedroom, over the sound of the shower, Siobhán calls out, "Is somebody there?"

Ron looks from the bedroom door to the front door. The knocking suddenly stops, and the doorknob slowly turns. The front door opens, and the man enters, carrying the duffel bag. He smiles and says, "Weren't locked."

It's the same man they saw at the pub earlier tonight, seconds before it was destroyed by the bomb. And it's the same man Ron saw back in December; the night the World's End was blown apart. In the basement apartment, the man's red hair looks like fire.

He closes the door and locks it. When he moves to place the duffel bag on the coffee table, the brothers flinch, fearing another bomb. But it lands with a dull thud and not a blast.

He turns to the brothers. "Fancy a drink?"

"We don't drink."

The man cocks a wry smile and walks toward the small kitchen as the brothers retreat to the couch. Noisily searching in a cupboard for a bottle and glass, he says, "You boys sure seem to spend a lot of time in pubs. For people who don't drink, I mean."

The man opens the freezer portion of the refrigerator and takes out a few ice cubes. He tosses the ice into a tall glass and fills it up halfway with whiskey. He carries the whiskey to one of the rattan chairs and sits down, exhaling loudly.

"Tough day?" Russell says with a sneer.

The man ignores this and takes a long sip, slurping the whiskey like it's his morning coffee.

The brothers examine him more closely. The man looks to be in his late twenties. His pale skin is marked by freckles, some so large they look like moles. His eyes are dark green, almost the same color as Dinky's Humber. His clothes are cheap but fashionable.

"We know who you are," Ron finally says.

"I know you do." The man takes another large sip. "Nasty bit of business tonight."

"Then why did you cause it?" Russell says.

The man just shrugs and puts his feet up on the coffee table. His feet are small; the green shoes look like avocados with laces. In the next room, the shower stops. They hear Siobhán hum as drawers are opened and closed. She calls out, "Be there in a minute, boys!"

"Look," Russell says quietly, "whatever you want with us, leave the girl out of it."

"Yeah," adds Ron, "we'll go with you, but promise you won't lay a hand on her."

The man just smiles and says, "Oh, I'm going to put my hands *all* over her."

Ron makes a fist and is standing up when the bedroom door opens. He sits back down when he sees Siobhán enter the living room. Instead of a sexy nightgown, or nothing at all, she's wearing a tan trench coat tied at the waist over dark slacks. She's carrying a pink hard-shell suitcase and on her head is a black beret.

"Boys," she says, "meet Clive."

She puts down the suitcase near the coat rack and leans in to give Clive a kiss. Both Ron's and Russell's stomachs turn. This is worse than being in the speedboat. Siobhán goes to the kitchen and comes back a minute later with a whiskey to match Clive's. She sits in the other rattan chair.

Looking slowly from Clive to Siobhán, Russell says, "You set us up."

Ron turns to his brother and asks, "What do you mean?"

"Don't you see? At the hotel. They needed someone to make that fake call. She was there scouting for a decoy." To Siobhán, he says, "You weren't in Beckenham this morning doing an errand. You were looking for chumps."

Taking a sip, Clive adds, "And she found them."

"We didn't need both of you," Siobhán says. "But you seemed like a package deal."

Clive leans over and kisses her again.

"She did all right, she did."

"Was it worth it?" Ron says. "Maiming all those people? Just to make your point, to spread your meaningless propaganda?"

Clive and Siobhán laugh. When he finishes his drink, she goes to the kitchen to make him another.

"Propaganda?" he says, still laughing. "Mate, you've got me all wrong. I'm from Bethnal Green, not Belfast."

Clive leans forward and unzips the duffel bag. Once again, the brothers recoil, thinking it contains either explosives or firearms. Instead, it's stuffed with cash. The brothers see red and purple and orange and green. American money all looks the same, the identical shade of pale gray and light yellow. But British pounds resemble a rainbow.

"You see," says Clive, "in a back room of that pub we hit tonight is the local bookie. The blast was just to cause a distraction while we did him in for a pretty penny. Clever, ain't it?"

Siobhán rejoins them, handing Clive his drink.

Russell turns to her and asks, "You're okay with this?"

She sits down and lights a cigarette.

"I told you before, I'm not going to be a secretary forever."

"And that's why it wasn't a problem for your boss," says Ron. "You never told him."

Siobhán grins and asks, "Why would I? I knew you two were barking up the wrong tree."

"Did you do the same thing at King's Road?" Ron asks Clive bitterly. "How much did you make that time?"

Clive sits up slightly and crosses his arms. His pale face turns a shade of red, almost matching his hair.

"How do you know about the World's End?"

"We were there."

Clive's defensiveness suddenly melts, the cocky grin returns.

"Nah, that wasn't nothing like this. That was the real thing. I almost got killed—bleeding Irish." He takes a sip of the whiskey. "But it made me start to think there has to be a better way."

"So you came up with the idea for all this." Ron kicks at the coffee table.

"Not bad, eh? The way I figure it, those IRA blokes will get the blame and we get off scot-free. Why, that bookie won't even go to the police. It's genius."

There's noise in the courtyard, people walking by. Clive stiffens and reaches into his blazer. But the footsteps pass. Relieved, he turns to Siobhán.

"Honey, did you tell them who used to live here? Maybe the fellas will get a kick out of that."

"No," she says, absentmindedly, taking a long drag on her cigarette. "I didn't tell them."

"The Krays," Clive says. "Not this exact unit, mind you, but the complex. Cedra Court. Flats right on top of each other."

Ron asks, "Who are the Krays?"

"Ronnie and Reggie Kray," Clive says, his voice dripping with admiration. "Best gangsters London's ever seen. They're doing porridge now but, in their prime, they were something else. And they was brothers, just like you. Twins."

"We're not twins," Russell says.

"Or criminals," adds Ron.

"No," says Clive, "but you look out for each other. If you hadn't, you wouldn't be alive right now. That's the thing about brothers."

The more he talks, the more Ron and Russell notice Clive's Cockney accent. "Thing" comes out *fing* and "brothers" sounds like *brovvers*.

While Clive drains the last of his drink and Siobhán stubs out her cigarette, Ron stands up slowly.

"Well, it's been a fun evening, but we'll be on our way."

"Sorry, mate." Clive puts down his empty glass. "We can't let you leave. You know too much."

Russell thinks he's bluffing. "You wouldn't."

"Look, if I was prepared to destroy a whole pub for a few thousand quid, you don't think I'd do you in just so's we can make a clean getaway?"

"Oh, and where are you going?"

Siobhán pulls out from under a copy of *Petticoat* the bulging envelope she had that morning. The tickets to Spain.

"My boss can catch the next trip."

"Flight leaves at midnight," Clive says. "So I'm afraid we need to be moving things along here."

He stands up, reaches into his blazer, and pulls out a black Luger. Waving it toward the bedroom, he says, "Let's go. Into the tub, both of you. Single file, and no funny business."

Russell stands and leads the way. Ron follows.

The brothers are just entering the bedroom when Ron turns quickly, slams the door, and locks it. Clive instantly starts banging on the door with the heel of the pistol.

"Let me in, you goddamn poofter!"

Russell runs into the bathroom, looking for an escape. The small room is still steamy from Siobhán's shower. There's a slim, rectangular opening above the medicine chest, but it's too small for anyone to fit through, even Russell. He darts back into the bedroom.

Ron's struggling to open a window in the corner, near the bedside table. The window overlooks the alley, with the apartment building's parking lot just beyond. But the window won't open; the old wood is warped. Russell helps his brother try to get it open. From the living room, Clive announces he's going to shoot his way in on the count of three.

Ron and Russell continue to struggle with the window, only it's hard to get a good grip or any kind of leverage.

"One!"

Ron finally steps back and kicks aside the bedside table. Siobhán's jewelry, a lamp, and pile of paperback books crash to the floor. This allows Ron to lean in and put his shoulder right up under the middle joist.

"Two!"

With their combined strength, the window finally opens with a crack. Ron grabs Russell, pushing him into the alley.

"Three!"

Ron's just going through the window when the shots begin. He looks back to see Clive blast away the lock and half the door.

The brothers sprint to the end of the alley. The parking lot's to their left and the courtyard leading to Cazenove Road—the way they came before—is on their right. Fearing that the parking lot might lead to a dead end, Ron leads Russell back toward the street.

"Freeze!"

The brothers face half a dozen points of light. It feels to Russell like being onstage: the glare of the spotlights, an eager crowd just beyond. But it's just a few flashlights.

Policemen suddenly jump out of doorways and bushes. They run from police cars just pulling up to the curb in front of the apartment building.

Ron and Russell raise their arms to protect themselves from the bullets or the blows they're sure are going to follow. But the officers all run right past them, on their way to the basement apartment. They're not after the brothers.

Stunned, Ron and Russell stumble forward. Parked amid the police cars, they see Dinky and the Humber.

"Had a funny feeling when we dropped you off earlier," Dinky says, getting out of the car. "Thought you might need reinforcements."

By the time the police are done with Ron and Russell, it's almost eleven. Dinky's long gone. He had a two-hour drive ahead of him, and he wasn't quite sure the Humber would make it. If he was going to break down, he wanted it to be early enough so that he could hitch a ride the rest of the way. Ron and Russell thanked him once again and assured the drummer they'd see him the next day in the studio, except this time they would meet him there. Tomorrow they're going to take the bus.

The brothers ended up in the back of a police car telling a sergeant everything they knew. It was the first time they'd been in a cop car since getting pulled over outside Houston, years ago, on their first tour. They told the policeman about getting kidnapped from the hotel, the phone call, the house in the suburbs, the escape on the speedboat, and what happened at the pub. The sergeant took it all down in a small black notebook, only occasionally interrupting to ask a follow-up question or request more detail. When Russell inquired about the smuggler, suggesting maybe some divers and a police boat could save the man, the sergeant chuckled and said the fish had already made him their dinner.

The brothers were hesitant to tell the sergeant too much about Siobhán. They thought maybe she would get off easy for only being an accessory and, if so, they could see her either after she got out of jail or after they were finished recording their album, whichever came first. But the sergeant said she'd be going away for a long time. The pub tonight hadn't been the first time Clive and Siobhán pulled such a stunt. There had been two prior bombings in the spring, with associated robberies, and they were already planning a fourth.

As the brothers sat there, telling their story, the sergeant kept receiving updates and reports. The blue van had been found, and the men from the house in the suburbs were in custody. It turns out they were all indeed IRA, and they weren't happy to have been used. They'd been out looking for Clive, armed to the teeth, only they got pulled over first. As they were being taken in, they relayed a message: they'd be waiting for him in Broadmoor.

The police even picked up the three gangsters. When the goons took Archie to a hospital in Notting Hill for the bullet in his leg, the doctor on call didn't quite believe their story about a hunting accident. The police were summoned. It turned out the trio were known to the local authorities and were wanted for a variety of crimes. They were arrested without incident, but not before the doctor prescribed Rocco something for his cold.

Even Clive and Siobhán gave themselves up without a fight. The only shots that ended up being fired that night were the ones at the bedroom door. As they were being led away in handcuffs, Siobhán locked eyes with Russell and mouthed, "Call me."

Closing the notebook, the sergeant says, "Thank you again for your cooperation. Are you sure I can't have one of our officers give you a ride back to Beckenham?"

The brothers step out of the vehicle.

"No thanks," says Russell. "We've spent too much time in the back of cars today."

"We're just going to walk," adds Ron. "At least for a bit. Then we'll catch a cab."

The sergeant tucks the notebook into his back pocket and goes to relieve the last officer on the scene.

Earlier, after the shots and when the police were raiding the basement flat, it seemed that every tenant had come out to see what the commotion was. For those who'd been around when Ronnie and Reggie Kray lived there, it brought back all kinds of exciting memories. But now Cedra Court is quiet. Only a few of the building's many windows are lit up by lamps or flickering TVs. Everyone else is asleep.

Ron and Russell walk to the corner and turn onto the large street. There's not much traffic and the shop windows are dark, except for an off-license on the corner. Passing by, they see a Pakistani man behind a counter reading the *Daily Mail*.

For a long time neither brother speaks, they just walk. First one block, then two, then three.

"That pier today," Ron finally says. "Where we brought in the speedboat."

"Brighton. What about it?"

"Reminded me of Santa Monica. Where Dad used to take us fishing for perch."

Russell smiles and says, "I can still see the painting he did of it."

"Never did like the taste of the fish we caught."

"Me neither."

They turn a corner. Most of the left side of the short block is covered with a wooden fence. Through holes in the barrier are views of a cement foundation, exposed rebar, and huge tools sitting idly under the moonlight. Almost the whole fence is covered with posters and handbills. Advertisements for concerts, cigarettes, greyhound races at Hackney Wick Stadium. Toward the end, as the brothers slowly pass, familiar faces peer back at them. Their own.

It's an ad for their first single on Island. There's a picture of Dinky, Ron, Russell, and Martin Gordon and Adrian Fisher, the bassist and guitarist who played on *Kimono My House*. Adrian's facing away from the camera. The print, slightly faded, is still readable under a streetlamp. *The Smash Single by* SPARKS. *England's Hottest New American Group.*

Ron points to the poster and says, "Propaganda."